"A fierce hand-to-hand fight was in progress."

# SOLDIERS OF THE QUEEN

BY

## HAROLD AVERY

# SOLDIERS OF THE QUEEN.

## CHAPTER I.

### TIN SOLDIERS.

"They shouldered arms, and looked straight before them, and wore a splendid uniform, red and blue."— *The Brave Tin Soldier.*

The battle was nearly over. Gallant tin soldiers of the line lay where they had fallen; nearly the whole of a shilling box of light cavalry had paid the penalty of rashly exposing themselves in a compact body to the enemy's fire; while a rickety little field-gun, with bright red wheels, lay overturned on two infantry men, who, even in death, held their muskets firmly to their shoulders, like the grim old "die-hards" that they were. The brigade of guards, a dozen red-coated veterans of solid lead, who had taken up a strong position in the cover of a cardboard box, still held their ground with a desperate valour only equalled by the dogged pluck of a similar body of the enemy, who had occupied the inkstand with the evident intention of remaining there until the last cartridge had been expended.

Another volley swept the intervening stretch of tablecloth, and the deadly missiles glanced against the glass bottles and rattled among the pencils and penholders. Two men fell

"Another volley swept the intervening stretch of tablecloth."

without a cry, and lay motionless with their heads resting on the pen-wiper.

"Look here, Barbara, you're cheating! You put in more than two peas that time, I know."

It was the commander-in-chief of the invading forces who spoke, and the words were addressed to a very harum-scarum looking young lady, who stood facing him on the opposite side of the table.

"How d'you know I did?" she cried.

"Because I saw them hit. There were three at least, and the rule was that we weren't to fire more than two at a time."

"There weren't three, then," retorted the girl, laughing, and shaking back her tangled locks with an impatient movement of her head. "There were *six*! Ha! ha! I put them all in my mouth at once, and you never noticed."

"Oh, you little cheat!" cried the boy. "I'll lick you."

The threat had evidently no terrors for her. She danced wildly round the table, crying, "Six! six! six!" and when at length he caught her, and held her by the waist, she turned round and rapped him smartly on the head with a tin pea-shooter.

At this stage of the proceedings a lady, who had been sitting in a low chair by the fire, looked up from her book.

"Come, come!" she said pleasantly. "I thought the day was past when generals fought single combats in front of their men. Isn't that true, Valentine?"

The tussle ceased at once; the boy released his sister, who laughed, and shook herself like a small kitten.

"She's been cheating!" he exclaimed.

"I fired six peas instead of two!" cried the culprit, evidently delighted with her little piece of wickedness. "And I knocked over two of his silly old soldiers."

A girl, somewhat older than Valentine, though very like him in face, laid down her needlework, saying, with a quiet smile,—

"All's fair in love and war, isn't it, Barbara?"

"Yes, of course it is," answered her sister.

"It's not—is it, aunt?" retorted the boy.

The lady rose from her chair, and, with a merry twinkle in her eye, came over to the table.

"Well, we'll hope not," she said. "Why, Val, I should have thought you were too old to play with tin soldiers; you were fourteen last birthday."

"I don't think I shall ever be tired of playing with them—that is," he added, "until I'm with real ones."

"Queen Mab," as the children sometimes called her, was below the medium height, and as she stood by her nephew's side his head reached above the level of her shoulder. She glanced over the mimic battlefield, and then down at the bright, healthy-looking young face at her side, with its honest grey eyes and resolute little mouth and chin. The old words, "food for powder," came into her mind, and she laid her hand lightly on his rumpled hair.

"So you still mean to be a soldier?"

"Yes, rather; and father says I may."

Miss Fenleigh was silent for a moment. "Ah, well," she said at length, "a happy time will come some day when there will be no more war; and I think it's about time this one ceased, for Jane will be here in a minute to clear the table for tea."

If Valentine or either of his sisters had been asked to describe their Aunt Mabel, they would probably have done so by saying she was the best and dearest person in the world; and accepting this assertion as correct, it would be difficult to say more. Her house also was one of the most delightful places which could well be imagined; and there, since their mother's death, the children spent each year the greater part of their summer holidays.

It was a dear, easy-going old house, with stairs a little out of the straight, and great beams appearing in unexpected places in the bedroom ceilings. There were brass locks with funny little handles to the doors, and queer alcoves and cupboards let into the walls. There was no fusty drawing-room, with blinds always drawn down, and covers to the chairs, but two cosy parlours meant for everyday use, the larger of which was panelled with dark wood which reflected the lamp and firelight, and somehow seemed to be ready to whisper to one stories of the days when wood was used for wall-paper, and when houses were built with sliding panels in the walls and hiding-places in the chimneys. The garden exactly matched the house, and so did the flowers that grew in it—the pink daisies, "boy's love," sweet-williams, and hollyhocks, all of which might be picked as well as looked at. Visitors never had a chance of stealing the fruit, because they were always invited to eat it as soon as it was ripe, or even before, if they preferred.

There were a lawn, and a paddock, and a shrubbery, the last so much overgrown that it resembled a little forest, and often did duty for a miniature "merry Sherwood," when the present of some bows and arrows caused playing at Robin Hood and his men to become a popular pastime. Lastly, there was the stable, where Jessamine, the little fat pony, and the low basket-carriage were lodged; and above was the loft, a charming place, which had been in turn a ship, a fortress, a robbers' cave, and a desert island. Up there were loads of hay and bundles of straw, which could be built up or rolled about in; the place was always in a romantic twilight; there were old, deserted spiders' webs hanging to the roof, looking like shops to let, which never did any business; and the ascent and descent of the perpendicular ladder from the ground floor was quite an adventure in itself. To picture a ship on which one had to go aloft to enter the cabin would seem rather a difficult task; but a child's imagination is the richest in the world, and though Valentine and his sisters had grown rather too old for this style of amusement, every fresh visit to Brenlands was made brighter by recollections of the many happy ones which had preceded it, and of all the fun and frolic they had already enjoyed there.

But best and foremost of all the charming things which made the place so bright and attractive was Queen Mab herself. She never said that little people ought to be seen and not heard; and there never was a person so easy to tell one's troubles to, or so hard to keep a secret from, as Aunt Mabel. No one in the world could ever have told stories as well as she did. "The Brave Tin Soldier" and "The Ugly Duckling" were the favourites, and came in time to be always associated with Brenlands. They had been told so often that the listeners always knew exactly what was coming next, and had the narrator put the number of metal brethren at two dozen instead of twenty-five, or missed out a single stage of the duckling's wanderings, she would have been instantly tripped up by her audience. But Queen Mab was too skilful a story-teller to leave out the minutest detail in describing the perilous voyage of the paper boat, or to spare the duckling a single snub from the narrow-minded hen or the bumptious tom-cat. The "Tin Soldier" she generally gave in answer to the special request of her small nephew, but she herself seemed to prefer the other story. There, the duckling's sorrowful wanderings finished with his turning into a swan, and Queen Mab always had a liking for happy endings.

She and the old house were exactly suited to each other, and seemed to share the same fragrant atmosphere, so that wherever her courtiers met her, and flung their arms round her neck, they were instantly reminded of sweet-brier and honeysuckle, jars of dried rose leaves, and all the other delicious scents of Brenlands. The children never noticed that there were streaks of silver in her hair, or that on her left hand she wore a mourning ring; nor did they know the reason why, on a certain day in the year, she seemed, if possible, more kind and loving than on any other, and went away somewhere early in the morning with a big bunch of flowers, and came back with the basket empty.

"Aunt," said Barbara, "what's an old maid?"

"Why, I'm one!" answered Queen Mab, laughing; whereupon it became every one's ambition to live a life of single blessedness. When there was cherry-tart for dinner, an alarming number of stones were secretly swallowed, in order that the person guilty of this abominable piece of sharp practice might count out, "This year—Next year—Some time—Never!" and at old maid's cards the object of the game was now reversed, and instead of trying to "go out," every one strove to remain in, the fortunate being in whose hands the "old maid" remained at the finish always brandishing the hitherto detested card with a shriek of triumph.

The last trace of the mimic battle had been cleared away, and now where tin cavalry had ridden boldly to their fate, and lead guards had died but not surrendered, nothing was to be seen but peaceful plum-cake, or bread and butter cut in thin and appetizing slices.

"I'm sorry you weren't able to make a longer stay," said Aunt Mabel, as she poured out the tea. "But your father said he couldn't spare you for more than a week at Easter. However, the summer will soon be here, and then you will come again for a proper visit. By-the-bye, Valentine, d'you know that your cousin Jack is coming to be a school-fellow of yours at Melchester?"

"No, aunt; is that Uncle Basil's son?"

"Yes; I want you to make friends with him, and bring him over here on your half-term holiday. I hope he will come for a few weeks at midsummer, and then you will all be able to have a jolly time together."

"How old is he?" asked Valentine.

"Oh, I think he is about a year older than you are—fifteen or thereabouts."

Barbara had fished a stranger out of her cup, and was smiting the back of one plump little hand against the other, to the accompaniment of "Monday—Tuesday—Wednesday," and so on.

"Aunt Mab," she said suddenly, "how is it we never hear anything of Uncle Basil, or that he never comes to visit us? What's Jack like?"

"Well, I can hardly tell you," replied Miss Fenleigh; "I've only seen him once, poor boy, and that was several years ago."

"But why don't we ever see Uncle Basil?" persisted Barbara. "You often come and visit us, and why doesn't he?"

"Well, I live within ten miles of your house, and Padbury is thirty or forty miles on the other side of Melchester."

"But that isn't very far by railway; and if he can't come, why doesn't he write?"

Aunt Mabel seemed perplexed what reply to make, but at this moment the boy came to her rescue.

"Don't ask so many questions, Bar," he said.

Miss Barbara was always ready for a tussle, with words or any other weapons. "Pooh!" she answered, "whom d'you think you're talking to? I know what it is, you're angry because I knocked over more of your soldiers than you did of mine!"

"Yes, you cheated."

"Fiddles! You thought I'd only got two peas in my mouth, you old stupid, and instead of that I'd got six, *six*! ha! ha!" And so the discussion continued.

Helen was nearly two years older than Valentine. She was a quiet, thoughtful girl, and later in the evening, when her brother and sister had gone to bed, she remained talking with her aunt in front of the fire. While so doing, she returned to the subject of their conversation at the tea-table.

"Aunt, why is it that father and Uncle Basil never meet?"

"Well, my dear, I didn't like to talk about it before Val and Barbara; it's a pity they should hear the story before they are older and can understand it better; besides, I wish the boys to be good friends when they meet at school. Basil and your father had a dispute many years ago about some money matters connected with your grandfather's will, and I am sorry to say they have never been friends since. Your uncle has always been a very unpractical man; he has wasted his life following up ideas which he thought would bring him success and riches, but which always turned out failures. He always has some fresh fad, and it always brings him fresh trouble. I don't think he would wilfully wrong any one, but from being always in difficulties and under the weather, his temper has been soured and his judgment warped, and he cannot or will not see that your father acted in a perfectly just and honourable manner, and the consequence is, as I said before, they never made up their quarrel."

"And Jack is going to the school at Melchester?"

"Yes; and I want Valentine to make friends with him, and for us to have him here in the summer. Poor boy, soon after your mother died, he lost his, and I am afraid his life and home surroundings have not been very happy since. Well, we must try to brighten him up a bit. I've no doubt we shall be able to do that when we get him here at Brenlands."

# CHAPTER II.

## AN UGLY DUCKLING.

"They had not been out of the egg long, and were very saucy. 'Listen, friend,' said one of them to the duckling, 'you are so ugly that we like you very well.'"—*The Ugly Duckling.*

It was the first day of term, and Melchester School presented a general appearance of being unpacked and put together again, as though the whole institution had been sent out of town for the holidays, and had returned by goods train late on the previous evening. The passages were strewn with the contents of boxes belonging to late comers; new boys wandered about, apparently searching for something which they never found; while the old stagers exchanged noisy greetings, devoured each other's "grub," and discussed the prospects of the coming thirteen weeks which they must pass together before the commencement of the summer vacation.

Most of the boys had arrived on the Monday evening, but Valentine Fenleigh did not come back until the following morning. According to a promise made to his aunt before leaving Brenlands, one of the first things he did was to inquire after his cousin.

"Yes," said one of his classmates, "there is a new chap by the name of Fenleigh, but I don't know what he's like. He's not put with us in the Lower Fourth."

Among a hundred and fifty boys, and in the confusion of a first day, it was a difficult matter to discover at once the whereabouts of the fellow he wanted. He accosted one or two of the new-comers, but by the time the bell rang for afternoon school he had only succeeded in ascertaining the fact that his cousin must be somewhere about, from having seen the name "J. Fenleigh" ticked off on the bedroom list.

Holms was full of a project for hiring a bicycle during the summer months, and, what with listening to the unfolding of this plan, and struggling with the work in hand, Valentine soon forgot the existence of his undiscovered relative.

Towards the end of the first hour Mr. Copland, the form-master, folded up a piece of paper on which he had been writing, and handing it across the desk, said,—

"Fenleigh, take this in to Mr. Rowlands, and bring back an answer."

Valentine made his way to the head-quarters of the Upper Fourth. The classroom was rather quieter than the one he had left, Mr. Rowlands being somewhat of a martinet.

"All right," said the latter, who was copying a list of questions on the blackboard; "put your note on my table, and I'll attend to you in a moment."

The messenger did as he was told, and stood looking round the room, exchanging nods and winks with one or two members of the upper division with whom he was on friendly terms.

On a form at the back of the room sat three boys who were hardly ever seen apart, and who had apparently formed an alliance for the purpose of idling their time, and mutually assisting one another in getting into scrapes. Their names were Garston, Rosher, and Teal; and seated at the same desk was a boy with whom they seemed to have already struck up an acquaintance, though Valentine did not remember having seen his face before. Even in the Upper Fourth there was a subdued shuffle, showing that work was going rather hard on this first day; and the young gentlemen whose names have just been mentioned were evidently not throwing themselves heart and soul into the subject which was supposed to be occupying their undivided attention.

Mr. Rowlands finished a line, made a full stop with a sharp rap of his chalk, and then turned round sniffing.

"Dear me!" he said, "there's a strong smell of something burning."

"Perhaps it's Jackson's cricket cap," murmured a small boy. Jackson's hair, be it said, was of a fiery red, and hence the suggestion that his head-gear might be smouldering in his pocket.

"What's that?" demanded Mr. Rowlands, and the joker subsided.

Jackson waited until a fresh sentence had been begun on the blackboard; then he dropped a ruler, and in picking it up again smote the small boy on a vulnerable spot beneath the peak of his shell-jacket.

"There *is* something burning," repeated the master. "Has any one of you boys got matches in his pocket?"

"Oh, *no*, sir!" shouted a dozen voices.

"Answer more quietly, can't you? I'm not deaf! Jackson, see if there's anything in the stove."

The stove was found to contain nothing but a bit of ink-sodden blotting-paper. Jackson drew it carefully forth, and held it up between his finger and thumb. "That's all, sir," he said.

"Then put it *back*, sir," cried the master, "and go on with your work."

Valentine had some difficulty in keeping from laughing. The smell which had greeted Mr. Rowlands' nostrils was caused by Garston, who was deliberately burning holes with a magnifying glass in the coat of the boy in front of him, who sat all unconscious of what was happening to this portion of his wardrobe.

The new fellow, who watched the proceedings with great interest, now stretched out his hand, and taking the glass held it up level with the victim's neck.

A moment later there was a yell.

"Who made that noise?"

"Please, sir, somebody burnt my neck!"

15

"Burnt your neck! What boy has been burning Pilson's neck?"

The new-comer raised his hand and gave a flip with his thumb and finger. "I did," he answered.

"You did!" exclaimed Mr. Rowlands wrathfully. "What are you thinking of, sir? I've spoken to you four times to-day already. I don't know if you were accustomed to behave in this manner at the last school you were at, but let me tell you—"

"Please, sir," interrupted Pilson plaintively, "they've burnt a hole in my back!"

At this announcement the class exploded.

"*Silence!*" cried the master. "What do you mean, Pilson? is your coat burnt?"

"Yes, sir."

"Very well, Fenleigh; I shall give you five hundred lines."

Valentine, who had been an unoffending spectator of the affair, was fairly staggered at suddenly hearing himself commissioned to write five hundred lines. Then the situation dawned upon him—this reckless gentleman with the burning-glass was his cousin Jack.

Mr. Rowlands made a memorandum of the punishment, and at the same time scribbled a few words in reply to Mr. Copland. As he did so, Valentine had an opportunity of examining his relative's appearance. The latter might have been pronounced good-looking, had it not been for a perpetual expression of restlessness and discontent, which soured what would otherwise have been a pleasant face. He seemed to care very little for the lines, and as soon as the master's eye was off him he turned to Garston and winked.

Valentine was by no means what is commonly known as a "good boy;" he was as fond of a lark as any right-minded youngster need be; but he had been taught at home that any one who intended to become a soldier should first learn to obey, and to respect the authority of those set over him. He did not like plunging into rows for the sake of being disorderly; and something in Jack Fenleigh's careless behaviour did not tend to leave on his mind a very favourable impression of his newly-found cousin. He had, however, promised Queen Mab to make friends; and so, as soon as afternoon school was over, he waited for Jack in the gravel playground, and there introduced himself.

"Oh, so you're Valentine," said the other. "My guv'nor told me you were here."

"Yes. I hope we shall be friends."

"Well, there's no reason why we shouldn't. My guv'nor's had a row with yours, I know; but that's nothing, he's always quarrelling with somebody, and I'm sure I don't mind, if you don't. By-the-bye, weren't you the fellow who was in the classroom when I got into that row about the burning-glass?"

"Yes; and I say it's rather a pity you go on like that the first day you're here. Masters don't expect new fellows to begin larking at once, and you'll get into Rowlands' bad books."

"Oh, I don't mind that," answered the other; "I didn't want to come here, and I don't care if I'm sent going again."

At this moment Garston joined them.

"Hallo!" he said, "are you two related to each other? I never thought of your names being the same before. Cousins, eh? Well, look here, new Fenleigh, Pilson's on the war-path after you for burning his neck."

"I don't care if he is," answered the other.

Hardly had the words been spoken when the subject of them turned the corner.

"Yes," he cried, "you're the chap I'm after! What did you burn my coat for?"

"I didn't burn your coat."

"Oh, you liar! Look here, I'm just going to—"

What Pilson *was* going to do will remain for ever unknown. He had no sooner laid his hand on Jack's collar than the latter, without a moment's hesitation, struck him a heavy blow on the chest which sent him staggering back against the wall gasping for breath.

"Just keep your dirty paws off me. I tell you I didn't burn your coat; though to look at it, I should think burning's about all it's good for."

This was not at all the usual line of conduct which new boys adopted when brought to book by an oldster. Pilson felt aggrieved, but made no attempt to follow up his attack.

"All right," he said. "You're a liar, and I'll tell all the other fellows."

"You can tell 'em what you please," returned the other, and taking hold of Garston's arm he walked away.

Valentine turned on his heel with a doubtful look on his face; his cousin evidently knew how to take care of himself, yet the latter's conduct was not altogether satisfactory. It was Garston who had burnt the coat, and it was like him to let another boy bear the blame; while Jack evidently cared as little for being thought a liar as he did for any other misfortune that might befall him.

During the next few days the cousins met every now and again in the playground, or about the school buildings, but it was only to exchange a nod or a few words on some subject of general interest. There seemed to be little in common between them; and Jack, though willing enough to be friendly and forget the family feud, evidently found the society of the three unruly members of the Upper Fourth more to his liking than that of a steady-going boy like Valentine.

For nearly a month the latter did his best to form the friendship which his aunt had desired; then an event happened which caused him to almost regard the task as hopeless. Jack had been steadily winning for himself the reputation of a black sheep; but the climax was reached when he further distinguished himself in connection with certain extraordinary proceedings known and remembered long afterwards as the "Long Dormitory Sports."

It was Rosher's idea. The chamber in question was called "Long" from the fact that it contained sixteen beds, eight on a side, all of which were occupied by members of the Upper Fourth. Skeat, the Sixth Form boy in charge, was ill, and had gone to the infirmary; and in the absence of the proverbial cat, the mice determined to get in as much play as possible, only stopping short at performances which might attract the attention of the master on duty.

It was one Tuesday night. Garston and Teal had had a quarter mile walking race up and down the centre aisle, which had ended, to the great delight of the spectators, in Garston nearly tearing his nightshirt off his back by catching it on a broken bedstead, while the other competitor had kicked his toe against an iron dumb-bell, and finished the race by dancing a one-legged hornpipe in the middle of the course, while his opponent won "hands down."

"I say," remarked Rosher, "why shouldn't we have proper sports, with a proper list of events and prizes?"

"Who'll give the prizes?" asked Teal.

"Oh, anybody! Look here. I vote we have sports to-morrow night before old Skeat comes back. Hands up, those who are agreeable! To the contrary!—none. Very well, it's carried!"

"But how about prizes?" persisted Teal, who was of rather a mercenary disposition.

"There needn't be any proper prizes," answered Rosher; "we can give the winners anything."

"Give 'em lines," suggested Garston.

"No; shut up, Garston. Everybody must give something. I'll offer a brass match-box, shaped like a pig."

"No, you won't," interrupted Teal. "It's mine; you borrowed it a week ago, and never gave it me back."

"Did I? Well, I'll tell you what, I'll offer a photograph of my brother; the frame's worth something. Now, what'll you give, Garston?"

Garston offered a small pocket-mirror. Jack Fenleigh a bone collar-stud, while a boy named Hamond promised what was vaguely described as "part of a musical box," and which afterwards turned out to be the small revolving barrel, the only fragment of the instrument which remained.

Prizes having been secured, the next thing was to arrange competitions in which to win them; and in doing this, the committee were obliged to keep in view the peculiar nature and limitations of the ground at their disposal. It was no good Hamond's clamouring for a pole jump, or Teal suggesting putting the weight. Jack's proposal of a sack race in bolster cases was, for a moment, entertained as a good idea; then it was suddenly remembered that the bolsters had no cases, and so that project fell through.

One by one the events were decided on. Rosher promised to draw up a programme, and insisted that after every boy's name some distinguishing colours should appear, as on a proper sports list, and that competitors were to arrange their costumes accordingly.

"When shall it come off?" asked Garston.

"Oh, to-morrow, after the masters have all gone in to supper. Now, we've been planning long enough; good-night."

The occupants of the Long Dormitory, be it said to their credit, were not fellows to form a scheme and then think no more about it, and the next day their minds were exercised with preparations for the sports, the chief difficulty being in arranging costumes which should answer to the descriptions given on Rosher's card. These vagaries in dress caused an immense amount of amusement, and when the masters' supper-bell gave the signal for the commencement of operations, every one found it difficult to retrain from shouts of laughter at the sight of the various styles of war-paint. Perhaps that of Jack Fenleigh, though simple to a degree, was most comical: his colours were described as "red and white," and his costume consisted of his night-shirt, and a large scarlet chest-protector which he had borrowed from a small boy, whose mother fondly believed him to be wearing it according to her instructions, instead of utilizing it to line a box containing a collection of birds' eggs.

As every race had to be run in a number of heats the events were necessarily few in number. There were a hopping race, a hurdle race over the beds, and a race in which the competitors were blindfolded, and each carried a mug full of water, which had not to be spilt by the way.

Teal, over whose bed, as the result of a collision, two boys happened to empty the contents of their half-pint cups, professed not to see much fun in the performance, though every one else voted it simply screaming.

But the contest looked forward to with the greatest amount of interest was the obstacle race. It was placed at the end of the programme; Garston's pocket-mirror, the only prize worth having, was to reward the winner; and the conditions were as follows:—

The runners were to go once round the room, alternately crawling under and hopping over the sixteen beds; the finish was to be down the middle aisle, across the centre of which a row of chairs was placed, on which boys stood or sat to keep them steady while the racers crawled under the seats. In spite of the fact that the pocket-mirror was to be the prize, only Jack and Hamond appeared at the starting-point when it came to this last item on Rosher's programme, their companions voting it too much fag, and preferring to sit on the obstacles and look on.

The signal was given, and the two competitors started off in grand style, plunging in and out among the beds like dolphins in a choppy sea. Jack led from the first; he dashed up to the row of chairs a long way in front of Hamond, and had wriggled the greater portion of his body through the bars, when—

No one could have said exactly how the alarm was given, or who first saw the gleam of light through the ground-glass ventilator. The obstacle was snatched from the centre of the room; with a rush and a bound everybody was in bed; a moment later Mr. Rowlands entered the room, the first thing which met his gaze being the extraordinary spectacle of Jack Fenleigh, who, like a new kind of snail, was crawling along the floor on his hands and knees with a cane-bottomed chair fixed firmly on the centre of his back. The weight of the boy sitting on it being removed, the unfortunate Jack found it impossible to force his way any further, and thus remained unable to extricate himself from between the bars of the obstacle.

"Fenleigh," said the master, "get up off the ground. What are you doing, sir?"

The boy struggled to his feet, and in doing so revealed the glories of the chest-protector. There was a subdued titter from the adjacent beds.

"Silence!" cried Mr. Rowlands. "So you're responsible for this noise and disorder, Fenleigh? If you want to perform as a clown, you had better leave school and join a circus. At nine o'clock to-morrow you will come with me to the headmaster's study."

By breakfast-time on the following morning the story of this tragic finish to the obstacle race was all over the school. Valentine heard it, and waited anxiously to learn his cousin's fate. The latter escaped with a severe reprimand, and the loss of the next two half-holiday afternoons; but he was reminded that his conduct, especially for a new boy, had been all along most unsatisfactory, and he was given clearly to understand that any repetition of this constant misbehaviour would result in his being expelled without further warning.

"I wish you'd take more care what you're up to, Jack," said Valentine. "You're bound to get thrown out if you don't behave better."

"What's the odds if I am? I've only been here a month, and I hate the place already."

"It seems to me," answered Valentine sadly, "that you don't care a straw for anything or anybody."

"Well, why should I?" returned the other. "You wouldn't, if you were in my place."

# CHAPTER III.

## THE REBEL RECLAIMED.

"'I think he will grow up pretty, and perhaps be smaller; he has remained too long in the egg, and therefore his figure is not properly formed;' and then she stroked his neck and smoothed the feathers."—*The Ugly Duckling.*

Towards the end of June, Queen Mab wrote asking the two boys to come over for their usual half-term holiday.

"I'm not going," said Jack.

"Why not?" asked Valentine, astonished that any one should decline an invitation to Brenlands. "Why ever not? You'd have a jolly time; Aunt Mabel's awfully kind."

"I daresay she is, but I never go visiting. I hate all that sort of thing."

It was no good trying to make Jack Fenleigh alter his mind; he stuck to his resolution, and Valentine went to Brenlands alone.

"I'm sorry Jack wouldn't come with you," said Queen Mab on the Saturday evening; "why was it? Aren't you and he on good terms with each other?"

"Oh, yes, aunt, we're friendly enough in one way, but we don't seem able to hit it off very well together."

"How is that?"

"Oh, I don't know. I'm not his sort; I suppose I'm too quiet for him."

"I always thought you were noisy enough," answered Miss Fenleigh laughing.

"You wouldn't, if you knew some of our fellows," returned the boy.

The weeks slipped by, the holidays were approaching, and the far-off haven of home could almost, as it were, be seen with the naked eye. Whether the disastrous termination to the dormitory sports had really served as a warning to Jack to put some restraint upon his wayward inclinations, it would be difficult to say; but certainly since the affair of the obstacle race he had managed to keep clear of the headmaster's study, and had only indulged in such minor acts of disorder as were the natural consequences of his friendship with Garston, Rosher, and Teal. It needed the firm hand of Mr. Rowlands to hold in check the sporting element which at this period was, unfortunately, rather strong in the Upper Fourth, and which, at certain times—as for instance during the French lessons—attempted to turn the very highroad to learning into a second playground.

Monsieur Durand, whose duty it was to instil a knowledge of his graceful mother tongue into the minds of a score of restless and unappreciative young Britons, found the facetious gentlemen of the Upper Fourth a decided "handful." They seemed to regard instruction in the Gallic language as an unending source of merriment. Garston threw such an amount of eloquence into the reading of the sentence, "My cousin has lost the hat of the gardener," that every one sighed to think that a relative of one of their classmates should have brought such sorrow on the head of the honest son of toil; and when Teal announced joyfully that "His uncle had found the hat of the gardener," Rosher was obliged to slap the speaker on the back, and say, "Bravo!"

This being M. Durand's first term in an English school, that gentleman could hardly have been expected, as the saying goes, to be up to all the moves on the board; and certain of his pupils, sad to relate, were only too ready to take advantage of his lack of experience. It was discovered that it was comparatively easy to obtain permission to leave the class. "Please, sir, may I go and get a drink of water?" or "Please, sir, may I go and fetch my dictionary?" was sufficient to obtain temporary leave of absence; nor did the French master seem to take much notice as to the length of time which such errands should by right have occupied. The consequence was that not unfrequently towards the end of the hour a quarter of his pupils were gathered in what was known as the playshed, drinking sherbet, or playing cricket with a fives ball and a walking-stick.

One particular morning, when the Lower Fourth were struggling with the parsing and analysis of a certain portion of Goldsmith's "Deserted Village," a mysterious patch of light appeared dancing about on the wall and ceiling, attracting the attention of the whole class, and causing the boy just told to "go on" to describe "man" as a personal pronoun, and to put a direct object after the verb "to be."

"Fenleigh," said Mr. Copland, "just see who that is outside."

Valentine, who was seated nearest the window, rose from his place, and looking down into the yard beneath saw the incorrigible Jack amusing himself by flashing sunbeams with the pocket-mirror which he had won in the dormitory sports. The latter, who ought by rights to have been transcribing a French exercise, grinned, and promptly bolted round the corner.

"Who was it, Fenleigh?"

Valentine hesitated.

"Who was it? Did you see the boy?"

"Yes, sir; it was my cousin."

"What! J. Fenleigh in the Upper Fourth?"

"Yes, sir."

"Humph! very well," answered Mr. Copland, making a memorandum on a slip of paper in front of him; "I'll seek an interview with that young gentleman after school."

Valentine's heart sank, for he had in his pocket a letter from Queen Mab saying that she was driving over in the pony carriage that very afternoon, and inviting the two boys to spend their half-holiday with her in Melchester. This significant remark of Mr. Copland's meant that Jack would be prevented from going. Valentine felt that he was indirectly the cause of the misfortune, and his wayward relative seemed inclined to view the matter in the same light.

"I say," he exclaimed, "you were a sneak to tell Copland it was I who was flashing that looking-glass."

"I couldn't help it," answered Valentine. "He told me to look out and see who was there."

"Well, why didn't you say the fellow had run away, or something of that sort?"

"Because it would have been a lie."

"Pooh! telling a cram like that to a master doesn't count. You are a muff, Valentine," and the speaker turned on his heel with a contemptuous shrug of his shoulders.

The little fat pony, the low basket-carriage, Jakes the gardener driving, and last and best of all Queen Mab herself, arrived at the time appointed; but only one of her nephews was waiting at the rendezvous.

"Why, where's Jack?"

"He got into a scrape this morning, and is kept in. What's more, he says it's my fault, and we've had a row about it. I don't think we ever shall be friends, aunt."

"Oh, you mustn't say that. In a fortnight's time we shall all be at Brenlands together, and then we must try to rub some of the sharp corners off this perverse young gentleman. I must come back with you to the school and try to see him before I drive home."

In the quiet retirement of Mr. Copland's classroom, Jack was writing lines when a messenger came to inform him that some one wished to see him in the visitors' room.

"Bother it! Aunt Mabel," he said to himself. "I suppose I must go," he added, swishing the ink from his pen and throwing it down on the desk. "What a bore relations are! I wish they'd let me alone."

From their one brief meeting years before, neither aunt nor nephew would have recognized each other now had they met in the streets, and so this was like making a fresh acquaintance. Jack had heard only one half of a very

27

lopsided story, and though he took no interest in the family disagreement, yet he was inclined to be suspicious of his grown-up relations. He marched down the passage, jingling his keys with an air of defiance; but when he entered the visitors' room, and saw the bright smile with which his aunt greeted his appearance, he dropped the swagger and became stolidly polite. She, for her part, had come prepared for the conquest which she always made; his awkward, boyish manner and uncared-for appearance, the dissatisfied look upon his face, and the ink stains on his collar, all were noticed in one loving glance, and touched her warm heart.

"Well, Jack," she said, "you see Mahomet has come to the mountain. How are you, dear?"

Jack muttered that he was quite well. It was rather embarrassing to be called "dear." He attempted to hide his confusion by wiping his nose; but in producing his handkerchief, he pulled out with it a forked catapult stick and a broken metal pen-holder, which clattered to the ground and had to be picked up again.

"How you've grown!" said Queen Mab, "and—my senses! what muscles you've got," she added, feeling his arm.

Jack grinned and bent his elbow, the next moment he straightened it again.

"Go on!" he said; "you're chaffing me."

"I'm not. I wish you'd been at Brenlands at Easter, and I'd have set you to beat carpets. Never mind, I shall have you with me in a fortnight."

"I don't think I shall come," he began.

"Stuff and nonsense!" interrupted the aunt. "I say you *are* coming. Valentine never makes excuses when I send him an invitation. Don't you think I know how to amuse young people?"

"Oh, yes; it's not that."

"Then what is it?"

"I don't know," answered the boy, grinning, and kicking the leg of the table.

"Of course you don't; so you've got to come. Valentine's sisters will be there; you'd like to meet the two girls?"

"No, I shouldn't."

"Oh, shocking! you rude boy."

Jack stood on one leg and laughed; this was like talking to a fellow in the Upper Fourth, and his tongue was loosed.

"They'd hate me," he said; "I don't know anything about girls."

"I should think you didn't. Wait till you see Helen and Barbara."

"But there's another thing. I haven't got any clothes."

"My dear boy, how dreadful! Whose are those you are wearing now?"

"Oh, go on, aunt; what a chaff you are! I don't mean that—I—"

"No, you evidently don't know what you mean. Well, one thing's settled, you're coming to Brenlands for the summer holidays."

The battle was won, and Queen Mab had gained her usual victory.

"How is your father? Didn't he send me any message?"

"Yes, I think he told me to give you his love."

"Is that all?"

"Well, that's a jolly sight more than what he sends to most people," answered the boy.

He would have been surprised to have seen that there were tears in her eyes when she walked out of the school gates, and still more astonished to know that it was love for his unworthy self which brought them there; for little did Fenleigh J. of the Upper Fourth imagine that any one would come so near to crying on his account.

That evening, just before supper, Valentine felt some one touch him on the shoulder, and turning round saw that it was his cousin.

"I've seen Queen Mab, as you call her," remarked the latter, "and, I say—I like her—rather."

"I knew you would. She's an angel—only jollier."

"She made me promise I'd go there for the holidays."

"Oh, that's fine!" cried Valentine. "I thought she would; she's got such a way of making people do what she wants. I am glad you are going; you'll enjoy it awfully."

Fenleigh J. regarded the speaker for a moment with rather a curious glance. In view of the events of the morning he rather expected that his cousin would not be overpleased to hear that he had been asked to spend the holidays at Brenlands; and that Valentine should rejoice at his having accepted the invitation, struck him as being rather odd.

"Look here, Val," he blurted out, "I'm sorry I called you a sneak this morning. It was my fault, and you're a good sort after all."

"Oh, stop it!" answered the other. "I'll forgive you now that you've promised to go to Brenlands."

Queen Mab was at home, miles away by this time; yet, as a result of her flying visit, some of the softening influence of her presence and kindly usages of her court seemed to linger even amid the rougher and more turbulent atmosphere of Melchester School.

# CHAPTER IV.

## THE COURT OF QUEEN MAB.

"They were swans ... the ugly little duckling felt quite a strange sensation as he watched them."—*The Ugly Duckling.*

During the short period which elapsed between Queen Mab's visit and the end of the term Jack managed to steer clear of misfortune; but on the last evening he must needs break out and come to grief again.

He incited the occupants of the Long Dormitory to celebrate the end of work by a grand bolster fight, during the progress of which conflict a pillow was thrown through the ventilator above the door. It so happened that, at that moment, Mr. Copland was walking along the passage; and a cloud of feathers from the torn case, together with fragments of ground glass, being suddenly rained down on his unoffending head, he was naturally led to make inquiries as to the cause of the outrage. As might have been expected, Fenleigh J. was found to be the owner of the pillow which had done the damage, and he was accordingly kept back on the following day to pay the usual penalty of an imposition.

"I'll take your luggage on with me," said Valentine. "You get out at Hornalby, the first station from here, and it's only about a quarter of a mile from there to Brenlands. Any one will tell you the way."

It turned out a wet evening. Queen Mab and her court had already been waiting tea for nearly half an hour, when Valentine exclaimed, "Hallo! here he is!"

The expected guest took apparently no notice of the rain; his cloth cricket cap was perched on the back of his head, and he had not even taken the trouble to turn up the collar of his jacket. He walked up the path in a cautious manner, as though he expected at every step to trip over the

31

wire of a spring-gun; but when he came within a dozen yards of the house he quickened his pace, for Aunt Mabel had opened the door, and was standing ready to give him a welcome.

"Why, boy, how late you are! You must be nearly starving!"

"I couldn't come before," he began; "I had some work to do, and—"

"Yes, you rascal! I've heard all about it. Come in, and Jane shall rub you down with a dry cloth."

Jack left off jingling his keys; he did not like being "rubbed down," but he submitted to the process with great good-humour. It was the cosiest old kitchen; the table was the whitest, and the pots and pans the brightest, that could be imagined; and Jane, the cook, groomed him down as though brushing a damp jacket with a dry glass-cloth was the most enjoyable pastime in life. In the parlour it was just the same: the pretty china cups and saucers, and the little bunches of bright flowers, only made all the nice things there were to eat seem more attractive; and the company were as happy and gay as though it was everybody's birthday, and they had all met to assist one another in keeping up the occasion with a general merry-making. Jack alone was quiet and subdued, for the simple reason that he had never seen anything like it in his life before.

Queen Mab, strongly entrenched at the head of the table, behind the urn, sugar basin, and cream jug, held this line of outworks against any number of flank attacks in the shape of empty cups, the old silver teapot apparently containing an inexhaustible supply of ammunition, and enabling her to send every storming party back to the place from whence it came, and even invite them to attempt another assault.

Once or twice Jack turned to find his aunt watching him with a look in her eyes which caused his own face to reflect the smile which was on hers. She was thinking, and had been ever since she had seen the latest addition to her court coming slowly up the front path through the dismal drizzle, of the old favourite story, and of that part in it where the ugly duckling, overtaken by the storm, arrived in front of the tumble-down little cottage, which "only remained standing because it could not decide on which side to fall first."

When the meal was over, and while the table was being cleared, Jack wandered out into the porch, and stood watching the rain. He had hardly been there a minute before he was joined by Barbara.

"I say," she exclaimed, "why didn't you talk at tea time? I wanted to ask you heaps of things. Your name's Jack, isn't it? Well, mine's Barbara; they call me Bar, because it's the American for bear, and father says I am a young bear. I want to hear all about that pillow fight, and those races you had in the dormitory."

"Oh, they weren't anything! How did you get to hear about them?"

"Why, Val told us."

"Well, what a fellow he is! He's always talking about the rows I get into."

"It doesn't matter; we thought it awful fun. Helen laughed like anything, and she's very good. I say, can you crack your fingers?"

"No; but I can crack my jaw."

"Oh, do show me!"

Jack really did possess this gruesome accomplishment; he could somehow make a blood-curdling click with his jawbone. When he did it in "prep." his neighbours smote him on the head with dictionaries, and when he repeated the performance in the dormitory, fellows rose in their beds and hurled pillows and execrations into the darkness. Barbara, however, was charmed.

"You are clever!" she cried; "I wish I could do it. Now, come back, and sit by me; we're going to play games."

Jack, who had cherished some vague notion that every girl was something between a saint and a bride-cake ornament, was agreeably surprised at this conversation with his small admirer, and readily complied with her request. Several of the games he had never seen before, but he made bold attempts to play them some way or another, and soon entered into the spirit of his surroundings.

In making words out of words his spelling was nearly as bad as Barbara's, but he seemed to think his own mistakes a great joke, and didn't care a straw how many marks he gave to the other players. In "Bell and Hammer," however, he always managed to buy the "White Horse," while other people would squander their all in bidding for a card which perhaps turned out after all to be only the "Hammer." At "Snap" he was simply terrible; he literally swept the board, but kept passing portions of his winnings under the table to Barbara, whose pile seemed to be as inexhaustible as the widow's cruse. By the end of the evening he was the life of the party, and no one would have believed that he was the same boy who, a few hours ago, had come up the front path wishing in his secret heart that he was safely back at Melchester writing lines in the Upper Fourth classroom.

He and Valentine shared a delightful, old four-post bed, which in times gone by had had the marvellous property of turning itself into a tent, a gipsy van, or a raft, which, though launched from a sinking ship in the very middle of a stormy ocean, always managed to bring its crew of distressed mariners safely to shore in time to answer Queen Mab's cheery call of "Tea's ready!"

"It is nice to be here," said Valentine, dropping his head upon the pillow with a sigh of contentment. "Aren't you glad you came?"

"Yes," answered Jack. "Aunt Mabel seems so jolly kind and glad to see you. I wish you hadn't told her about all those rows I got into; I don't think she'll like me when she knows me better."

"Oh, yes, she will! Don't you like Helen?"

"Yes; I think she has the nicest face I ever saw. But she's too good for me, Val, my boy. I think I shall get on better with Barbara; she's more like a boy, and I don't think I shall ever be a ladies' man."

Valentine laughed; the idea of Fenleigh J. of the Upper Fourth ever becoming a ladies' man was certainly rather comical.

"You'll like Helen when you get to know her. I wouldn't exchange her as a sister for any other girl in the kingdom. Well—good-night!"

That one evening at Brenlands had done more towards forming a friendship between the two boys than all the ninety odd days which they had already spent in each other's company. The next afternoon, however, they were destined to become still more united; and the manner in which this came about was as follows.

During the morning the weather held up, but by dinner time it was raining again.

"Bother it! what shall we do?" cried Valentine.

"I should think you'd better play with your tin soldiers," answered Helen, laughing. "They always seem to keep you good."

Valentine hardly liked this allusion to his miniature army being made in the hearing of his older schoolfellow, for boys at Melchester School were supposed to be above finding amusement in toys of any kind. The latter, however, pricked up his ears, and threw down the book he had been reading.

"Who's got any tin soldiers?" he asked. "Let's see 'em." The boxes were produced. "My eye!" continued Jack, turning out the contents, "what a heap you've got! I should like to set them out and have a battle. And here are two pea-shooters; just the thing!"

35

"You don't mean to say you're fond of tin soldiers, Jack?" said Aunt Mabel. "Why, you're much too old, I should have thought, for anything of that kind."

"I'm not," answered the boy; "I love tin soldiers, and anything to do with war. Come on, Val, we'll divide the men and have a fight."

The challenge was accepted. There was an empty room upstairs, and on the floor of this the opposing forces were drawn up, and a desperate conflict ensued. The troops were certainly a motley crew; some were running, some marching, and some were standing still; some had their rifles at the "present," and some at the "slope;" but what they lacked in drill and discipline, they made up in their steadiness when under fire, and Jack showed as much skill and resource in handling them as did their rightful commander. He set out his men on some thin pieces of board, which could be moved forward up the room, it having been agreed that he should be allowed to stand and deliver his fire from the spot reached by his advancing line of battle. Each group of these tag-rag-and-bobtail metal warriors was dignified by the name of some famous regiment. Here was the "Black Watch," and there the "Coldstream Guards;" while this assembly of six French Zouaves, a couple of red-coats, a bugler, and a headless mounted officer on a three-legged horse, was the old 57th Foot—the "Die-Hards"—ready to exhibit once more the same stubborn courage and unflinching fortitude as they had displayed at Albuera. Valentine held a position strengthened by redoubts constructed out of dominoes, match-boxes, pocket-knives, and other odds and ends. They were certainly curious fortifications; yet the nursery often mimics in miniature the sterner realities of the great world; and since that day, handfuls of Englishmen have built breastworks out of materials almost as strange, and as little intended for the purpose, and have fought desperate and bloody fights, and won undying fame, in their defence.

"I'm going to be this chap, who takes on and off his horse," said Jack. "Which is you?"

"Here I am," answered Valentine. "Now then, you fire first—blaze away!"

As he spoke he picked up the veteran captain of the solid lead guards, and set him down in the centre of the defending force, and so the battle commenced. It was still raging when Jane came to say that tea was ready; but the losses on both sides had been terribly severe. The invading army still pressed forward, though the "57th" were once more decimated by the withering fire; and nothing actually remained of the "Coldstream Guards" but a kettle-drummer of uncertain nationality, and a man carrying a red and green flag, which he might very possibly have captured from some Sunday-school treat. The opposite side were in no better plight: men were lying crushed under the ruins of the works which they had so gallantly defended; and hardly enough artillerymen were left to have pulled back, with their united efforts, the spring of one of the pea cannons. The leaders on both sides remained unscathed, and continued to brandish bent lead swords at each other in mutual defiance.

"Make haste! you've got one more shot," said Valentine.

The pea-shooter was levelled and discharged, the veteran lead captain tottered and tell, and thus the fight ended.

"Val, my boy, you're killed!" cried Jack. "No matter, it's the bed of honour, old chap!"

"Oh, I don't mind!" answered the other, laughing. "*C'est la guerre*, you know; come along. I'd no idea you were so fond of soldiers."

So they passed down to Queen Mab's merry tea-table, unsaddened by any recollections of the stricken field, or of the lead commander left behind among the slain.

The two boys talked "soldiering" all the evening; and the next morning, when breakfast was nearly over, and Helen ran upstairs to inquire if they meant to lie on till dinner-time, they were still harping away on the same subject. The door was standing ajar, and she heard their words.

"Don't move your knee," Jack was saying; "that's the hill where I should post my artillery."

"Yes, that's all right," answered Valentine; "but you couldn't shell my reserves if I got them down under cover of this curl in the blanket.—All right, Helen! down directly!"

The sun was shining brightly, the fine weather seemed to have come at last, and the question was how to put it to the best possible use.

"Why don't you children go and picnic somewhere?" said Queen Mab. "You can have Prince and the carriage, and drive off where you like, and have tea out of doors."

A general meeting was held in the hayloft directly after dinner for the purpose of discussing this important question. Jack won a still higher place in Barbara's affections by hauling himself up the perpendicular ladder without touching the rungs with his feet; and though knowing little or nothing about such things as picnics, he was ready with any number of absurd suggestions.

"Let's go to Pitsbury Common," said Barbara; "there's such a lot of jolly sandpits to roll about in, and we can burn gorse-bushes."

"Oh, no, don't let's go there!" answered Helen; "there's no place to shelter in if it comes on rain, and when you're having tea the sand blows about and gets into everything, so that you seem to be eating it by mouthfuls."

"It's so nice having it out of doors," persisted Barbara.

"Well, let's go out in the road and sit with our feet in the ditch, like the tramps do," said Jack. "I'll bring the tea in my sponge bag. Rosher used to carry it about in his pocket, full of water for a little squirt he was always firing off in the French class. Pilson had the sentence, 'Give me something to drink;' and as soon as he'd said it, he got a squirtful all over the back of his head, and Durand—"

"Oh, stop that!" said Valentine, laughing. "Look here! I vote we drive over to Grenford, and call on the Fosbertons, and ask them to lend us their boat; they'd give us lunch, and then we could take our tea with us up the river. It's not more than six miles."

"Don't let's go there," said Barbara. "I hate them."

"Is Raymond away?" asked Helen.

"Yes; didn't you hear Queen Mab say he was going to spend his holidays in London? Uncle James is rather a pompous old fellow, but we shan't have to go there except for lunch; and father said we ought to call on them while we're here; besides, it'll be jolly on the river. You know them, don't you, Jack?"

"Well, I've *heard* about them," answered the other. "I know that the guv'nor's sister married old Fosberton, and that he got a lot of money making tin tacks, or whatever it was; and now he fancies he's rather a swell, and says he's descended from William the Conqueror's sea-cook, or something of that sort. I don't want to go and see them; but I don't mind having some grub there, if they'll lend us a boat."

"My senses! you ought to feel very much honoured at the thought of going to lunch at Grenford Manor," said Helen, laughing.

"I'm sure I don't," answered her cousin. "I'd sooner have a feed in old 'Duster's' shop at Melchester."

"Well, that's what we'll do," said Valentine. "We'll take a kettle and some cups with us, and tea, and all that sort of thing, and go up the river as far as Starncliff, and there we'll camp out and have a jolly time."

With some reluctance the proposal was agreed upon. Had the company foreseen the chain of events which would arise directly and indirectly from this memorable picnic, they might have made up their minds to spend the day at Brenlands.

# CHAPTER V.

## AN UNLUCKY PICNIC.

"The tom-cat, whom his mistress called 'My little son,' was a great favourite; he could raise his back, and purr, and could even throw out sparks from his fur if it were stroked the wrong way."—*The Ugly Duckling.*

"Now, Jack, do behave yourself!" cried Valentine, as the basket-carriage turned through two imposing-looking granite gate-posts into a winding drive which formed the approach to Grenford Manor. Jack, as usual, seemed to grow particularly obstreperous just when circumstances demanded a certain amount of decorum, and at that moment he was kneeling on the narrow front seat belabouring Prince with the cushion.

"Well," he answered, turning round, "we must drive up to the door in style; if we come crawling in like this, they'll think we're ashamed of ourselves."

As he spoke, a curve in the drive brought the house into view. It was a big, square building, with not the slightest touch of green to relieve the monotony of the rigid white walls, and level rows of windows, which seemed to have been placed in position by some precise, mathematical calculation. A boy was lounging about in front of the porch, with his hands in his pockets, kicking gravel over the flower-beds.

"O Val! you said Raymond wasn't at home," murmured Helen.

"Well, Aunt Mab said he was going to London; he must have put off his visit."

Raymond Fosberton turned at the sound of the carriage-wheels, and sauntered forward to meet the visitors. He had black hair, and a very pink and white complexion. To say that he looked like a girl would be disparaging to the fair sex, but his face would at once have impressed a careful observer as being that of a very poor specimen of British boyhood.

"Hallo!" he said, without removing his hands from his pockets, "so you've turned up at last! You've been a beastly long time coming!"

He shook hands languidly with Valentine and the two girls, but greeted Jack with a cool stare, which the latter returned with interest. Grenford Manor was very different from Brenlands. Aunt Isabel was fussy and querulous, while Mr. Fosberton was a very ponderous gentlemen in more senses than one. He had bushy grey whiskers and a very red face, which showed up in strong contrast to a broad expanse of white waistcoat, which was in turn adorned with a massive gold chain and imposing bunch of seals.

"Well, young ladies, and how are you?" he began in a deep, sonorous voice, of which he was evidently rather proud. "How are you, Valentine? So this is Basil's son?— hum! What's your father doing now?"

"I don't know," answered Jack, glancing at the clock. "I expect he's having his dinner, though there's no telling, for we're always a bit late at home."

Mr. Fosberton stared at the boy, cleared his throat rather vigorously, and then turned to speak to Helen.

Lunch was a very dry and formal affair. Raymond spoke to nobody, his father and mother addressed a few words to Valentine and the girls, but Jack was completely ignored. The latter, instead of noticing this neglect, pegged away merrily at salmon and cold fowl, and seemed devoutly thankful that no one interrupted his labours by forcing him to join in the conversation.

"You may tell your father," said Mr. Fosberton to Valentine, "that I find his family are related to one of the minor branches of my own; I've no doubt he will be pleased to hear it. His father's sister married a Pitsbury, a second cousin of the husband of one of the Fosbertons of Cranklen. You'll remember, won't you?"

Valentine said he would, and looked scared.

The silver spoons and forks were all ornamented with the Fosberton crest—a curious animal, apparently dancing on a sugar-stick.

"What is it?" whispered Barbara to Jack.

"The sea-cook's dog," answered her cousin.

"But what's he doing?"

"He's stolen the plum-duff, and the skipper's sent him up to ride on a boom, and he's got to stay there till he's told to come down."

At last the weary meal was over.

"I suppose we may have the boat," said Valentine.

"Oh, yes. I'm coming with you myself," answered Raymond; which announcement was received by Miss Barbara with an exclamation of "Bother!" which, fortunately, was only overheard by Jack, who smiled, and pinched her under the table.

It did not take long to transport the provisions and materials from the pony-carriage to the boat, and the party were soon under way. It was a splendid afternoon for a river excursion. Raymond, who had not offered to carry a thing on their way to the bank, lolled comfortably in the stern, leaving the other boys to do the work, and the girls to accommodate themselves as best they could. He was evidently accustomed to having his own way, and assumed the position of leader of the expedition.

"Have you finished school?" asked Jack.

"I don't go to one," answered the other; "I have a private tutor. I think schools are awful rot, where you're under masters, and have to do as you're told, like a lot of kids. I'm seventeen now. I'm going abroad this winter to learn French, then I'm coming home to read for the law. I say, why don't you row properly?"

"So I do."

"No, you don't; you feather too high."

"There you go again," continued the speaker petulantly a few moments later; "that's just how the Cockneys row."

"Sorry," said Jack meekly. "Look here, d'you mind showing me how it ought to be done?"

Raymond scrambled up and changed places with Jack. "There," he said—"that's the way—d'you see? Now, try again."

"No, thanks," answered Jack sweetly, "I'd rather sit here and watch you; it's rather warm work. I think I'll stay where I am."

Raymond did not seem to relish the joke, but it certainly had the wholesome effect of taking him down a peg, and rendering him a little less uppish and dictatorial for the remainder of the journey.

At Starncliff the right bank of the river rose rocky and precipitous almost from the water's edge. There was, however, a narrow strip of shore, formed chiefly of earth and shingle; and here the party landed, making the boat fast to the stump of an old willow.

"We promised Queen Mab that we wouldn't be very late," said Valentine, "so I should think we'd better have tea at once; it'll take some time to make the water boil."

There is always some special charm about having tea out of doors, even when the spout of the kettle gets unsoldered, or black beetles invade the tablecloth. To share one teaspoon between three, and spread jam with the handle-end of it, is most enjoyable, and people who picnic with a full allowance of knives and forks to each person ought never to be allowed to take meals in the open. Jack and Valentine set about collecting stones to build a fireplace, and there being plenty of dry driftwood about, they soon had a good blaze for boiling the water. The girls busied themselves unpacking the provisions; but Raymond Fosberton was content to sit on the bank and throw pebbles into the river.

The repast ended, the kettle and dishes were once more stowed away in the boat, and Valentine proposed climbing the cliff.

"It looks very steep," said Helen.

"There's a path over there by those bushes," answered her brother. "Come along; we'll haul you up somehow."

The ascent was made in single file, and half-way up the party paused to get their breath.

"Hallo!" cried Jack, "there's a magpie."

On a narrow ledge of rock and earth at the summit of the cliff two tall fir-trees were growing, and out of the top of one of these the bird had flown. The children stood and watched it, with its long tail and sharp contrast of black and white feathers, as it sailed away across the river.

"One for sorrow," said Helen.

"I shouldn't like to climb that tree," said Valentine. "It makes my head swim to look at it, leaning out like that over the precipice."

"Pooh!" answered Raymond; "that's nothing. I've climbed up trees in much worse places before now."

Helen frowned, and turned away with an impatient twitch of her lips.

Jack saw the look. "All right, Master Fosberton," he said to himself; "you wait a minute."

They continued their climb, and reaching the level ground above strolled along until they came opposite the tall tree out of which the magpie had flown.

"There's the nest!" cried Jack, pointing at something half hidden in the dark foliage of the fir. "Now, then, who'll go up and get it?"

"No one, I should think," said Helen. "If you fell, you'd go right down over the cliff and be dashed to pieces."

"I know I wouldn't try," added her brother. "I should turn giddy in a moment."

"Will you go?" asked Jack, addressing Raymond.

"No," answered the other.

"Why, I thought you said a moment ago that you've climbed trees in much worse places. Come, if you'll go up, I will."

"Not I," retorted Raymond sulkily; "it's too much fag."

"Oh, well, if you're afraid, I'll go up alone."

"Don't be such a fool, Jack," said Valentine; "there won't be any eggs or young birds in the nest now."

"Never mind; I should like to have a look at it."

Fenleigh J. of the Upper Fourth was a young gentleman not easily turned from his purpose, and, in spite of Valentine's warning and the entreaties of his girl cousins, he lowered himself down on to the ledge, and the next moment was buttoning his coat preparatory to making the attempt.

For the first twelve or fifteen feet the trunk of the fir afforded no good hold, but Jack swarmed up it, clinging to the rough bark and the stumps of a few broken branches. The spectators held their breath; but the worst was soon passed, and in a few seconds more he had gained the nest.

"There's nothing in it," he cried; "but there's a jolly good view up here, and, I say, if you want a good, high dive into the river, this is the place. Come on, Raymond; it's worth the fag."

"Oh, do come down!" exclaimed Helen. "It frightens me to watch you." She turned away, and began picking moon daisies, when suddenly an exclamation from Valentine caused her to turn round again.

"Hallo! what's the matter?"

Jack had just begun to slip down the bare trunk, but about a quarter way down he seemed to have stuck.

"My left foot's caught somehow," he said. "I can't get it free."

He twitched his leg, and endeavoured to regain the lower branches, but it was no good.

"Oh, do come down!" cried Helen, clasping her hands and turning pale. "Can't any one help him?"

Jack struggled vainly to free his foot.

"Look here," he said in a calm though strained tone, "my boot-lace is loose, and has got entangled with one of these knots; one of you chaps must come up and cut it free. Make haste, I can't hang on much longer."

Valentine turned to Raymond.

"You can climb," he said; "I can't."

"I'm not going up there," answered the other doggedly, and turned on his heel.

Valentine wheeled round with a fierce look upon his face, threw off his coat, took out his knife, opened it, and put it between his teeth.

"O Val!" cried Helen in a choking voice, and hid her face in her hands. Only Barbara had the strength of nerve to watch him do it, and could give a clear account afterwards of how her brother swarmed up the trunk, and held on with one arm while he cut the tangled lace. Valentine himself knew very little of what happened until he found himself back on the grass with Helen's arms round his neck.

"I thought you couldn't climb," said Jack, a minute later.

"It's possible to do most things when it comes to a case like that," answered the other quietly. "Besides, I remembered not to look down."

That sort of answer didn't suit Fenleigh J.; he caught hold of the speaker, and smacked him on the back.

"Look here, Valentine, the truth is you're a jolly fine fellow, and I never knew it until this moment."

The party strolled on across the field.

"It's precious hot still," said Raymond; "let's go and sit under that hayrick and rest."

"We mustn't stay very long," Helen remarked as they seated themselves with their backs against the rick. "We want to be home in time for supper."

"We can stay long enough for a smoke, I suppose," said Fosberton, producing a cigarette case. "Have one. What! don't you chaps smoke? Well," continued the speaker patronizingly, "you're quite right; it's a bad habit to get into. Leave it till you've left school."

"And then, when you smoke before ladies," added Helen, "ask their permission first."

"Oh, we haven't come here to learn manners," said Raymond, with a snort.

"So it appears," returned the lady icily.

Fenleigh J., who had been smarting under that "Leave it till you've left school," chuckled with delight, and began to think that he liked Helen quite as much as Barbara.

At length, when Raymond had finished his cigarette, the voyagers rose to return to the boat. Jack enlivened the descent of the cliff by every dozen yards or so pretending to fall, and starting avalanches of stones and earth, which were very disconcerting to those who went before. On arriving at the shingly beach, he proposed a trial of skill at ducks and drakes, and made flat pebbles go hopping right across the river, until Valentine put an end to the performance by saying it was time to embark. The girls were just stepping into the boat when Helen gave an exclamation of surprise.

"Look!" she cried, pointing towards the top of the cliff, "where can all that smoke be coming from?"

"It's a heap of rubbish burning in one of the fields," said Raymond.

"There's too much smoke for that," said Jack. "It may be a barn or a house. Wait a moment; I'll run up and see. I shan't be more than five or six minutes." He started off, jumping and scrambling up the path; but almost immediately on reaching the summit he turned and came racing down again.

"What a reckless beggar he is;" said Valentine. "He'll break his neck some day. Well, what is it?"

Jack took a flying jump from the path on to the shingle.

"The rick!" he cried—"the one we were sitting under—it's all in a blaze!"

The boys and girls stood staring at one another with a horrified look on their faces.

"You must have done it with your matches, Raymond," said Helen.

"I didn't," returned the other. "It's the sun. Come on into the boat."

"You must have dropped your cigarette end," said Valentine. "We ought to find the owner of the hay and say who we are."

"You fool! I tell you it wasn't me," returned the other passionately. "Ricks often catch fire of their own accord. I'm not going to be made pay for what isn't my fault."

Valentine hesitated, and shook his head. Jack seemed ready to side with him; but Raymond jumped into the boat and seized the oars. "Look here!" he cried, "it's my boat, and I'm going. It you don't choose to come, you can stay."

The two boys had no alternative but to obey their cousin's demand. Jack took the second oar, while Valentine steered. Raymond was ready enough now for hard work, and pulled away with all his might, evidently wishing to escape as fast as possible from the neighbourhood of the burning rick.

"What are you pulling so fast for?" asked Jack; but "stroke" made no reply, and seemed, if anything, to increase the pace.

"Look out!" cried Valentine, as the boat approached an awkward corner, one side of which was blocked by the branches of a big tree which had fallen into the water. "Steady on, Raymond!" "Stroke," who did not see what was coming, and thought this was only another attempt to induce him to lessen the speed at which they were going, pulled harder than ever. Valentine tugged his right-hand line crying, "Steady on, I tell you!" but it was too late. There was a tremendous lurch which nearly sent every one into the river, the water poured over the gunwale, and something went with a sounding crack. Raymond's oar had caught in a sunken branch and snapped off short. His face turned white with anger.

"You cad!" he cried with an oath, "you made me do that on purpose."

"I didn't!" answered Valentine hotly; "and I should think you might know better than to begin swearing before the girls."

Helen looked frightened, but Barbara was sinking with laughter at the sight of Jack, who, on the seat behind, was silently going through the motions of punching Master Fosberton's head.

"Well, we can't go on any further," said the latter. "We must get the boat into that backwater and tie her up. Though it'll be a beastly fag having to walk to Grenford."

Dividing between them the things which had to be carried, the cousins made their way through a piece of waste ground studded with gorse-bushes, and gained the road, which ran close to the river. Barbara lingered behind to pick Quaker grass, but a few moments later she came racing after them and caught hold of Jack's arm.

"Hallo!" he said, "what's up? you look scared."

"So I am," she answered. "I saw a man's face looking at me. He was hiding behind the bushes."

"Fiddles!" answered Jack. "It was only imagination. Come along with me. I'll carry those plates."

Raymond Fosberton seemed bent on making himself as disagreeable as possible. He was still in a great rage about the broken oar, and lagged behind, refusing to speak to the rest of the party.

"We ought not to let him walk by himself," said Helen, after they had gone about a mile; "it looks as if we wanted to quarrel."

She stopped and turned round, but Raymond was nowhere in sight. They waited, but still he did not appear.

"He can't be far behind," said Valentine. "I heard him kicking stones a moment or so ago."

Jack walked back to the last bend in the road and shouted, but there was no reply.

"It's a rum thing," he said, as he rejoined his companions. "I wonder what has become of the beggar. I thought just then I heard him talking."

The boys shouted again, and Barbara drew a little closer to Jack. Whether the watching face was imagination or not, she had evidently been frightened.

"Surly brute! he has gone home by a short cut," said Jack. "Come along! it's no use waiting."

They had not gone very far when they heard somebody running, and turning again saw their missing cousin racing round the corner. His face was pale and agitated, and it was evident that something was the matter.

"Hallo! where have you been?"

"Nowhere. I only stopped to tie my shoe-lace."

"But you must have heard us calling?"

"I never heard a sound," answered Raymond abruptly, and so the matter ended.

The four Fenleighs were not at all sorry to find themselves free of their cousin's society, and bowling along behind Prince in the little basket-carriage. It was still more delightful to be back once more at Brenlands, and there, round the supper-table, to give Queen Mab an account of their adventures.

"I should like to know who that man was whom I saw hiding among the bushes," said Barbara.

"I should like to know what Raymond was up to when we missed him coming home," said Valentine.

"Yes," added Jack thoughtfully; "he was hiding away somewhere, for I could have sworn I heard his voice when I walked back to the corner."

# CHAPTER VI.

## A KEEPSAKE.

"He is my own child, and he is not so very ugly after all, if you look at him properly."—*The Ugly Duckling.*

The holidays passed too quickly, as they always did at Brenlands. Jack was no longer the ugly duckling. Whatever misunderstanding or lack of sympathy might have existed hitherto between himself and Valentine had melted away in the sunny atmosphere of Queen Mab's court; and since the incident of the magpie's nest, the two boys had become fast friends.

Soldiering was their great mutual hobby. They constructed miniature earthworks in the garden, mounted brass cannon thereon, fired them off with real powder, and never could discover where the shots went to. They read and re-read "A Voice from Waterloo," the only military book they could discover in their aunt's bookcase; and on wet days the bare floor of the empty room upstairs was spread with the pomp and circumstance of war. The soldiers had a wonderful way of concealing their sufferings; they never groaned or murmured, and, shot down one day, were perfectly ready to take the field again on the next, and so when the solid lead captain or die mounted officer who took on and off his horse was "put out of mess" by a well-directed pea, the knowledge that they would reappear ready to fight again another day considerably lessened one's grief at the sight of their fall. Perhaps, after all, lead is a more natural "food for powder" than flesh and blood, and so the only time tears were shed over one of these battles was one morning when Barbara surreptitiously crammed two dozen peas into her mouth, fired them with one prolonged discharge into the midst of Valentine's cavalry, and then fled the room, whereupon Jack sat down and laughed till he cried.

It would be difficult to say what it was that made Queen Mab's nephews and nieces like to wander out into the kitchen and stand by her side when she was making pastry or shelling peas; but they seemed to find it a very pleasant occupation, and in this, after the first week of his stay, Jack was not a whit behind the others.

He was sitting one morning on a corner of the table, watching with great interest his aunt's dexterous use of the rolling-pin.

"Well, Jack," she said, looking up for a moment to straighten her back, "are you sorry I made you come to Brenlands?"

"No, rather not; I never enjoyed myself so much before. I should like to stay here always."

"What! and never go home again?"

The moment that word was mentioned he was once more Fenleigh J. of the Upper Fourth.

"Home!" he said; "I hate the place. I've got no friends I care for, and the guv'nor's always complaining of something, and telling me he can't afford to waste the money he does on my education, because I don't learn anything. I do think I'm the most unlucky beggar under the sun. I've got nothing to look forward to. But I don't care. When I'm older I'll cut the whole show, and go away and enlist. Any road, I won't stay longer than I can help at Padbury."

Queen Mab smiled, and went on cutting out the covering for an apple-tart.

"I know you like soldiers," she said; "well, listen to this. Just before the battle of Waterloo, the father of Sir Henry Lawrence was in charge of the garrison at Ostend. He knew that some great action was going to take place, and wished very much to take part in it; so he wrote to Wellington, reminding him that they had fought together in the Peninsular War, and asking leave to pick out the best of the troops then under his command and come with them to the front. The duke sent him back this reply,—'That he remembered him well, and believed he was too good a soldier to wish for any other post than the one which was given to him.'"

"You're preaching at me," said Jack suspiciously; "it's altogether different in my case."

"No, I'm not preaching; I'm only telling you a story. Now go and find my little Bar, and say I've got some bits of dough left, and if she likes she can come and make a pasty."

Barbara came, and Jack assisted her in the manufacture of two shapeless little turn-overs, which contained an extraordinary mixture of apples, currants, sugar, and a sprinkling of cocoa put in "to see what it would taste like." But the boy's attention was not given wholly to the work, his mind was partly occupied with something else. He wandered over and stood at the opposite end of the table, watching Queen Mab as she put the finishing touch to her pie-crust, twisting up the edge into her own particular pattern.

"I don't see why people shouldn't wish for something better when they have nothing but bad luck," he said.

"I don't think people ever do have nothing but bad luck."

"Yes, they do, and I'm one of them. I hate people who're always preaching about being contented with one's lot."

"You intend that for me, I suppose," said his aunt, slyly. "All right; if you weren't out of reach I'd shake the flour dredge over you!"

"No, you know I don't mean you," said the boy, laughing. "And I have had one stroke of good luck, and that was your asking me to Brenlands."

He went away, and told Valentine the story of Colonel Lawrence.

"I didn't think she knew anything about soldiers."

"She's a wonderful woman!" said Valentine, solemnly. "She knows everything!"

The following morning, as the two cousins were constructing an advanced trench in a supposed siege of the cucumber-frame, Helen came out and handed her brother a letter. Valentine read it, and passed id on to Jack.

"What d'you think of that?" he asked.

The epistle was a short one, and ran as follows:—

"GRENFORD MANOR,
"*Tuesday.*
"DEAR VALENTINE,—I want five shillings to square the man whose hayrick we set fire to the other day. If you fellows will give one half-crown, I'll give the other. Send it me by return certain, or there'll be a row.—Yours truly,

"RAYMOND FOSBERTON."

"Pooh! I like his cheek!" cried Jack. "At the time he said it was the sun; and now he says, 'the hayrick *we* set on fire,' when he knows perfectly well it was entirely his own doing. I should think he's rich enough to find the five shillings himself."

"Oh, he's always short of money, and trying to borrow from somebody," answered Valentine. "The thing I don't understand is, what good five shillings can be; the man would want more than that for his hay."

"I don't understand Master Raymond," said Jack. "What shall you do?"

"Well, as we were all there together, I suppose we ought to try to help him out. The damage ought to be made good; I thought he would have got Uncle Fosberton to do that. I'll send him the money; though I should like to know how he's going to square the man with five shillings."

A description of half the pleasures and merry-making that went to make up a holiday at Brenlands would need a book to itself, and it would therefore be impossible for me to attempt to give an account of all that happened. The jollification was somehow very different from much of the fun which Fenleigh J. had been accustomed to indulge in, in company with his associates in the Upper Fourth; and though it was not a whit less enjoyable, yet after it was over no one was heard to remark that they'd "had their cake, and now they must pay for it."

On the last morning but one, when the boys came down to breakfast, they found Queen Mab making a great fuss over something that had come by post.

"Isn't it kind of your father?" she said. "Look what he's sent me!"

The present was handed round. It was a gold brooch, containing three locks of hair arranged like a Prince of Wales's plume, two light curls, and a dark one in the middle—Valentine's, Helen's, and Barbara's.

"He says it's to remind me of my three chicks when they are not with me at Brenlands."

"Mine's in the middle!" cried Barbara.

"You ought to have some of Jack's put in as well," said Helen.

The boy glanced across at her with a pleased expression.

"Oh, no," he answered, "not alongside of yours."

During the remainder of the morning he seemed unusually silent, and directly after dinner he disappeared.

"D'you know where Jack is?" asked Valentine.

"No," answered Helen; "he went out into the road just now, but I have not seen him since."

It was a broiling day, and the children spent the greater part of the afternoon reading under the shade of some trees in the garden. They were just sitting down to tea when their cousin reappeared, covered with dust, and looking very hot and tired. He refused to say what he had been doing, and in answer to a fire of questions as to where he had been he replied evasively, "Oh, only along the road for a walk."

"Look sharp!" said Valentine, bolting his last mouthful of cake, "we're going to have one more game of croquet. Come on, you girls, and help me to put up the hoops."

Jack, who in the course of his travels had acquired a prodigious thirst, lingered behind to drink a fourth cup of tea.

"You silly boy," said his aunt, "where have you been?"

"To Melchester."

"To Melchester! You don't mean to say you've walked there and back in this blazing sun?"

"Yes, I have. I wanted to get something."

"What?"

The boy rose from his chair, and came round to the head of the table.

"That's it," he said, producing a little screw of tissue paper from his pocket. "It's for you. It's only a cheap, common thing, but I hadn't any more money."

The paper was unrolled, and out came a little silver locket.

"I didn't want the others to see—you mustn't ever let any one know. There's a bit of my hair inside."

"Now, then, don't stay there guzzling tea all night!" came Valentine's voice through the open window.

"But, my dear boy, whatever made you spend your money in giving me such a pretty present?"

"I want," answered the boy, speaking as though half ashamed of the request he was making—"I want you to wear it when you wear the brooch; stick it somewhere on your chain. I should like, don't you know, to feel I'm one of your family."

"So you are," answered Queen Mab, kissing him. "So you are, and always will be—my own boy Jack!"

# CHAPTER VII.

## STRIFE IN THE UPPER FOURTH.

*"'You are exceedingly ugly,' said the wild ducks."—The Ugly Duckling.*

School was a great change after Brenlands. The rooms seemed barer, the desks more inky, and the bread and butter a good eighth of an inch thicker than they had been at the close of the previous term; but by the end of the first week our two friends had settled to work, and things were going on much the same as usual.

Considerable alterations had been made in the composition of the Upper Fourth. Most of the occupants of the front row of benches had got their remove, while a number of boys from the lower division, of whom Valentine was one, had come up to join Mr. Rowlands' class. The Long Dormitory was also changed, and Jack now found himself in Number Eight, sleeping in a bed next to that of his cousin.

Being thus so much thrown together, both in and out of school, it was only natural that the friendship which they had formed in the holidays should be still more firmly established. Only one thing acted as a drag upon it, and that was the fact of Jack's still finding a strong counter-attraction in the society of Garston, Rosher, and Teal.

The quartette began the term badly by being largely responsible for a disturbance which occurred in the dining-hall, when a clockwork frog was suddenly discovered disporting itself in Pilson's teacup; and it is probable that Jack would have continued to distinguish himself as a black sheep, in company with his three unruly classmates, had it not been for an unforeseen occurrence which caused him to make a change in his choice of friends.

As not unfrequently happens, the few original members of the Upper Fourth who had not been called upon to "come up higher" still clung to their old position at the bottom of the class, while the front benches were filled by their more industrious schoolfellows who had earned promotion. This state of affairs was not altogether pleasing to some of the old hands. In Garston's opinion, the ideal Form was one which would have no top, and where everybody would be bottom; and when the first week's "order" was read out, he remarked, concerning those new-comers who had won the posts of honour, that it was "like their blessed cheek," and that some of them wanted a licking. Teal was entirely at one with his chum in this opinion, and showed his approval of the latter's sentiments by laying violent hands upon the person of Hollis, the head boy, making a playful pretence of wringing his neck, and then kicking his bundle of books down a flight of stairs. Hollis, a weakly, short-sighted youth, threatened to complain to Mr. Rowlands; which course of action, as may be supposed, did not tend to increase his popularity with his new classmates.

The very next morning the dogs of war broke loose. The boys were construing the portion of Virgil which had been set them overnight. Garston, who came last, had floundered about for a few moments among the closing lines, giving vent to a few incoherent sputterings, and every one was impatiently awaiting the first tinkle of the bell.

"Yes, Garston," said Mr. Rowlands, "that's certainly up to your usual form—quite a brilliant display; I'll give you naught. Let me see: I set the lesson to the end of the page, and told you to go further if you could; has any one done any more?"

"I have, sir," said Hollis; "shall I go on?"

The master nodded, Hollis proceeded, and Valentine, who stood second, also followed in turn with a continuation of the translation. He had only got through a couple of lines when the bell rang, and the class was dismissed. Hardly had the door closed behind them, when Rosher and Teal charged along the passage and seized hold of Valentine and Hollis. The other boys crowded round in a circle.

"Look here, my good chap," said Teal, "in future you'll have to drop that; d'you hear?"

"Drop what?"

"Why, doing more work than what's set."

"But why shouldn't I?" said Hollis. "There's no harm in it; he didn't give us any marks."

"You young fool! don't you see that if you do more than what's set, he'll think we can all do the same, and make the lessons longer."

"Of course he will!" added several voices.

"Just you mind what you're up to," continued Teal, "or you'll get what you won't like."

"Pass on there! What are you waiting for?" cried Mr. Rowlands, appearing in the doorway of his classroom, and the gathering dispersed.

The following morning, as fate would have it, nearly the same thing happened again, only this time during the hour devoted to algebra.

"Has any one had time to do any of the next set of examples?" asked Mr. Rowlands. "If so, let him hold up his hand."

Only two boys held up their hands—Hollis and Valentine. There were murmurs of discontent at the back of the room, and several fists were shaken ominously.

Jack had not troubled to side with either party—it mattered very little to him whether the lessons were long or short, as he only did as much as he felt inclined—but, if anything, his sympathies lay with his less industrious comrades, who, he considered, had very good ground for feeling aggrieved with Hollis and his cousin.

"Look here, Val," he said, when they met at the close of morning school, "what d'you want to go and work so beastly hard for?"

"I don't."

"No, perhaps you don't, because you're clever; but you're always doing more than you're obliged to, and the other chaps don't like it, because they say it'll make Rowlands set longer pieces."

"Oh, that's all rubbish! It's simply because they're waxy with us for getting above them in class. I don't see why I should take my orders from Rosher and Teal, and only do what they like; and I don't intend to either."

"All right, my boy," answered Jack, carelessly. "Do what you like, only look out for squalls."

The latter piece of advice was not at all unnecessary; for soon after this, as the giver was strolling across the gravel playground, he heard his name called, and looking round saw his cousin hurrying after him with a scrap of paper in his hand.

"Look," he said; "I found this in my desk just now, and there was one just like it in Hollis's."

Jack took the paper. It was an anonymous note, printed in capitals to disguise the handwriting; and it ran as follows:—

"This is to give you fair warning, that if you will persist in doing more work than what is set, you'll get a thrashing. The rest of the class don't intend to get more work on your account, and so have decided not to put up with your nonsense any longer."

"It was Rosher or one of those chaps wrote it," said Jack. "You'd better look out; any one of them could give you a licking."

"They'd have to try first," answered Valentine, hotly.

His cousin laughed; the reply rather tickled his fancy.

Those concerned had not long to wait before matters came to a head. That same afternoon Mr. Rowlands set a history lesson for the following day. "Take the reign of Elizabeth," he said. "By-the-bye, there's a genealogical tree at the end of the chapter; get that up if you can."

The examination next morning was a written one, and the last question on the board was, "Show, by means of a genealogical tree, the connection between the Tudors and the Stuarts."

"Please, sir," said Garston, "you told us we needn't do that."

"I said you were to get it up if you had time," returned the master. "Haven't any of you done it?"

"Yes, sir," came from the front desk.

"Very well; let those who have learned it write it down."

"Val, my boy," said Jack, in his happy-go-lucky style, as they met in the dormitory to change for football, "you just keep your eyes open; you're going to get licked."

Valentine replied with a snort of defiance, and the subject was dropped. Tea was over, and in the short respite between the end of the meal and the commencement of "prep.," Jack was strolling down one of the passages, when his attention was attracted by a certain small boy who stood beneath a gas-jet scanning the contents of a small book, and occasionally scribbling something on a half-sheet of exercise-book paper. Suddenly the youngster flung down the book in a rage, and kicked it across the passage, whereupon Jack promptly cried, "No goal!"

"Hallo, little Garston!" he continued, "what's up with you?"

"Why, I've got to write out the translation of some of this Caesar for old Thorpe, and I can't make head or tail of the blessed stuff. I say, Fenleigh, you might do a bit for me!"

Jack was a good-natured young vagabond. "Where is it?" he said, picking up the book. "All right! here goes."

Garston Minor slapped his piece of paper up against the wall, and wrote at his friend's dictation. The translation was not very accurate, but coming from the lips of a fellow in the Upper Fourth it was accepted without question by the juvenile, and in ten minutes the rough copy of the imposition was finished.

"Thanks awfully!" said the youngster, as he stuffed the book and paper back into his pocket. "Look here, Fenleigh;

as you've done me a good turn, I'll let you into a secret, only you must promise not to let my brother know who told you. He and Teal and Rosher are going to give your cousin a licking."

"How d'you know?"

"I heard them talking about it. They said, 'We'll lick Valentine Fenleigh. If we touched Hollis, he'd sneak; but it'll frighten him if we thrash the other chap.'"

"When are they going to do it?"

"Now—some time; they said soon after tea."

"Where?" cried Jack.

"I can't tell you; they didn't say. That's all I know."

Jack exploded with wrath. He had talked calmly enough to Valentine about his getting licked, and was inclined to think he deserved it; but now that it had come to the point, he found that the idea of his cousin being thrashed was not at all to his liking. Even at that very moment the outrage might be taking place. The victim was not equal to any one of his three assailants, and stood much less chance of escaping from their combined attack.

Fenleigh J. rushed off down the passage on a wild-goose chase after his chum, but nowhere was the latter to be found. As a last resource, he ran into the schoolroom. Valentine's seat was empty, but a boy sat reading at the next desk but one.

"Have you seen my cousin?"

"Yes, he was here a minute ago."

"Where's he gone?"

"Bother you!—let's see—oh, I know; some one came in to say Darlton wanted him in the little music-room."

"Darlton never gives lessons after tea. Phew! I see what's up!"

The boy looked up from his reading with a grunt of astonishment as his questioner turned sharply on his heel and dashed out of the room. Jack had his faults, but he was loyal-hearted enough to remember those who had at any time proved themselves to be his friends, and not to leave them in the lurch when an opportunity offered for rendering them some assistance. He was a strong boy, but the back desk trio were also good-sized fellows for their age. Had it, however, been the whole of the Sixth Form who were licking Valentine, Jack in his present state of mind would have charged in among them and attempted a rescue.

"It's clear enough," he muttered to himself, as he turned off down a short, narrow passage; "that message was a trap to catch him alone. But wait a minute, and I'll surprise the beggars."

He paused outside a door, and hearing voices within tried the handle. It was locked.

"Hallo! who's there? You can't come in."

Jack was too wary to make any reply. He glanced round rapidly, endeavouring to concoct some plan for gaining an entrance. Stooping down, he discovered that the key was turned so that it remained exactly in the centre of the keyhole, anything pushed against it would send it out on the other side. "I believe that bathroom key fits this door," he muttered, and tiptoed a little further along the passage. In another moment he was back again, and thrusting the key suddenly into the lock he turned it, and forced open the door.

The room was a small chamber set apart for music practice, the only furniture it contained being a piano, a chair, some fiddle-cases, and music-stands, while on the mantelpiece, in the place of a clock, was a metronome that had something wrong with the works. Jack, however, had no eye for these details; his attention was centred in a group of boys who were struggling under the single gas-jet, which was flaring away in a manner which showed it had evidently been turned up in a hurry.

"Here, leave that chap alone!" he exclaimed, plunging into the centre of the scrimmage. "Let him alone, I say!"

"Hallo! it's Fenleigh J.," cried Garston. "You've just come in time to help us to teach this cousin of yours a lesson on the subject of not overworking himself."

"Leave him alone!" repeated Jack angrily, giving Rosher a push which sent him staggering back into the fireplace, where he knocked over the metronome, which fell with a crash on the fender.

"Don't be a fool, Fenleigh," cried Teal. "We're going to teach this chap a lesson. If you don't want to help, you can clear out."

"I shall do nothing of the sort," returned the other. "You let him alone."

Both parties were too much in earnest to waste their breath in talking, and the next moment Garston and Rosher sprang on the intruder and endeavoured to force him out of the room. Valentine, being unable to free himself from the muscular grasp of Teal, could render no assistance; but his cousin, whose blood was fairly up, struggled furiously with his two assailants. Round the room they went, like a circular storm, wrecking everything they came in contact with; music-stands went over with an appalling clatter, while the back of the solitary chair gave way with a crash as the three combatants fell against it. Suddenly a sharp voice sounded down the passage,—

"Now then, there! What's all that noise about?"

Teal released his hold of Valentine, and springing to the gas-jet turned out the light.

"*Cave!*" he whispered: "it's old Thorpe!"

It was impossible to continue the struggle in the darkness, and the tumult ceased.

"He's gone into Copland's classroom," continued Teal. "Quick! let's hook it before he comes back!"

A rush was made for the door.

"All right, Fenleigh; don't you think you're going to be friends with us any more."

"I've no wish to be," answered Jack. "If you want to finish this out any time, I shall be quite ready for you!"

"It was jolly good of you to stick up for me like that," said Valentine, as the two cousins hurried off towards the schoolroom.

"I should have been a mean cad if I hadn't," returned the other, laughing. "You don't think I've forgotten that affair of the magpie's nest, do you? I don't care a straw for any of those fellows, and if they want to fight, I'll take them on any day; but they'll have to lick me first before they talk about thrashing you."

In course of time the dispute between the two extremes of the Upper Fourth died a natural death. Mr. Rowlands did not increase the length of the "prep." lessons, and peace was restored. Garston and his two companions, however, did not forgive Jack for his interference with their plans. Regarding him, perhaps, as rather a hard nut to crack, they made no attempt to renew the combat, but evidently decided to cut him off from any future enjoyment of their society or friendship.

Jack, on his part, did not seem to take this loss very much to heart; it only induced him to become more chummy with Valentine, and, judging from the comparatively few times that his name was down for punishment, this change of associates seemed to be decidedly to his advantage. As the autumn advanced, and wet days became more frequent, the two boys took to doing fretwork in their spare time; and having purchased a rather large and complicated design for a kind of bracket bookcase, they conceived the happy notion of making it as a Christmas present for Queen Mab, and so worked away together, taking an immense amount of interest in their task.

Before the term ended a rather curious incident happened, insignificant in itself, but worthy of being recorded as bearing on more important events to be dwelt on at a later period in our story.

It wanted about three weeks to the holidays, and Jack and Valentine were returning from the ironmonger's, where they had been purchasing some sandpaper wherewith to put the finishing touches to their work.

"I wish it was midsummer instead of Christmas," the former was saying. "I don't want to go home. I'd much rather go to stay with Aunt Mab at Brenlands."

Valentine was about to reply, when both boys were surprised by a shabby-looking man suddenly crossing from the other side of the street and taking up his stand directly in their path. The stranger wore a battered brown hat, no necktie, and a suit of clothes which he might have stolen from some scarecrow.

"'Afternoon, young gents!" he said.

"Good afternoon," answered Jack shortly, stepping out into the road.

The stranger turned and walked at their side.

"You may not remember me, gents, but I'm Ned Hanks."

"I don't care who you are," answered Valentine; "I don't know you."

"Oh, but I know you, sir; it's Mr. Fenleigh I'm a-talking to. I thought, perhaps, you might like to stand me a drink."

"I say, just be off," cried Jack sharply, "here's old Westford coming."

The man fell back, and a moment later the two boys raised their caps to the headmaster. Mr. Westford acknowledged their salutation with a cold stare, which clearly showed that he had seen their late companion, and was wondering what business two of his pupils had to be talking with such a vagabond.

"I wonder who that fellow was!" said Jack.

"Oh, some tramp. I never saw him before."

"But he knew your name."

"Well, these beggars are up to all kinds of dodges," answered Valentine. "If we'd waited long enough, I daresay he'd have told me the names of all the family!"

# CHAPTER VIII.

## A BANQUET AT "DUSTER'S."

"It must have been the fault of the black goblin who lived in the snuff-box."—*The Brave Tin Soldier.*

At Easter, Jack and Valentine got their remove into the Fifth, and there became acquainted with a young gentleman who rejoiced in the name of Tinkleby.

Tinkleby was a comical-looking fellow of medium height; he wore nippers, and had a perpetual smirk on his lips.

"Hallo, you two Fenleighs!" he said, coming up to them on the second morning of the term; "I suppose you'll join our society."

"What society?" asked Jack.

"The Fifth Form Literary Society."

"What's it for?" asked Valentine. "We're neither of us very literary."

"Well, to tell you the truth, the society isn't either. It's kept up for the sake of having a feed at the end of every summer term."

"What?" cried Jack, laughing.

"If you'll listen a moment," said Tinkleby glibly, "I'll explain the whole matter in two words.

"The fellows in the Fifth used to run a manuscript magazine. Aston was the first editor, and he called it the 'Portfolio,' because it was bound up in the case of an old blotter that he bagged out of the reading-room. The chaps who contributed papers called themselves the Fifth Form Literary Society, and elected a secretary, treasurer, and president. Aston was so pleased with one of the numbers that he sent it to *The Melchester Herald* to be reviewed; but after waiting about six months for a notice to appear, he went down to the office, and the editor said that the manuscript was lost, and that Aston ought to have enclosed stamps if he wanted it returned. Godson, one of the prefects, said he saw a bit at Snell's the fish-shop, where they were using it to wrap up screws of shrimps; but that was all rot, and he only said it because the fellows in the Sixth were jealous. Well, then, it was suggested that the magazine should be printed, and the members subscribed towards bringing out the first number; but after they'd raked in all the money they could get, they found there wasn't enough for the purpose, so they decided to spend what they'd got in having a feed at 'Duster's,' and it was agreed it should be an annual affair.

"When I was made president I brought out two numbers of the 'Portfolio,' but in the second I wrote rather a smart thing on old Ward, and called it 'The Career of a Class Master.' It was really so good I thought he'd enjoy reading it, and so I got another fellow to show it him; but he didn't properly appreciate it, and cut up rough. He said he would overlook the personal allusions, but he really couldn't allow any fellow in his form to be so backward in spelling, and therefore I must borrow a spelling-book from one of the kids, and learn two pages a day until I improved. He used to hear me before we began first lessons. It was rather rough on the president of a literary society, making him stand up every morning and reel off two pages of 'Butter's Spelling-Book.' And that squashed the 'Portfolio;' fellows wouldn't send in any more papers, for fear they should be hauled up in the same manner.

"But they went on subscribing for the feed," continued Tinkleby, brightening up. "We didn't let that fall through. It comes off on the breaking-up day, after the old boys' match. The Sixth are always invited in to have supper with the swells; but I know a lot or them would much rather be with us having a blow-out at 'Duster's.' Well, that's the meaning of our literary society; the subscription is only two-pence a week, so you'd better join."

The two cousins promised they would do so. Every Monday morning, in the classroom, Tinkleby passed round an old missionary box, crying, "Now then! pay up, you beggars. No broken glass or brace buttons!" It was always a race to get the collection over by the time Mr. Ward entered the room; but the sprightly Tinkleby, who seemed to have undertaken the combined duties of president, secretary, and treasurer, hurried through it somehow; and each week the box grew heavier, and the hearts of the contributors lighter as they looked forward to the time when they should sit down to the long-expected banquet.

The term passed very pleasantly for Jack and Valentine; and what between cricket, bathing, and the prospect of spending the coming holiday at Brenlands, they had good reason for feeling contented and happy. Only one thing happened to disturb their peace of mind, and that an incident of rather a curious nature.

They were strolling back to the school one afternoon, and had got within twenty yards of the main entrance, when some one hurrying along behind them touched Jack on the shoulder, and looking round they found themselves once more confronted by the same shabby-looking man who had accosted them on a previous occasion.

"Beg pardon, Mr. Fenleigh," he began. "I'm Ned Hanks; you'll remember, sir. Maybe you've got a copper or two you can spare a poor fellow who's out of work."

"I've got no money to give away to beggars," said Jack; "and I tell you once more we don't know you."

"That's rather ungrateful, I calls it," answered the man. "I did you two gents a good turn last year, and got precious little for it. I might have made more out of the other party."

By this time they had reached the school-gates.

"Look here," broke in Valentine, "don't you bother us any more, or we'll put a policeman on your track. I don't understand a word of what you've been saying, and—"

"Stop, stop, Fenleigh!" interrupted a deep voice. "What's the meaning of this, pray?"

The two boys looked up and found they were standing in the presence of the headmaster.

"What's the meaning of this?" he repeated. "Who is this man you're talking to?"

There was a moment's silence, during which the seedy stranger slunk away, and disappeared round the corner.

"I ask who is this man you are speaking to?"

"I don't know, sir," answered Valentine.

"Nonsense!" retorted Mr. Westford sharply. "I saw you two boys holding a conversation with him once before. You must know who he is; answer my question immediately."

"He told us his name was Hanks," said Jack; "but we don't know him. He came up and spoke to us of his own accord."

"And, pray, what did he want to speak to you about?"

"I don't know, sir," answered Valentine—"that is—he wanted to beg some money."

"I don't understand your answer, Fenleigh," replied Mr. Westford. "I fear you are not telling me the truth—or, at all events, you are trying to keep something back which ought to come to my knowledge. There must be some reason for my having twice found you in conversation with that disreputable-looking fellow. Both of you will not go outside the school premises for a fortnight without special permission."

Jack stormed and raved, and threatened what he would do if they should encounter the tramp again; but of the two, Valentine felt the punishment far more acutely than his cousin. He was not accustomed to rows; and for a boy with his naturally high sense of honour, the mere thought that the headmaster suspected him of telling a falsehood was ten times worse than the fact of being "gated."

The term ran on, and at length the last day arrived; a day of perfect happiness, with no more work, and a letter by the first post from Queen Mab, saying that the pony-carriage would meet the train as usual at Hornalby station. The prize-giving, with the Mayor of Melchester in the chair, and Augustus Powler, Esq., M.P., and other grandees, upon the platform, was a very serious and formal business; the Past and Present match, in which Preston, the coming man in bowling, took seven wickets, and dear old Clayton, a bygone captain, lifted a ball over the roof of the pavilion, was certainly more interesting; but, at all events, in the opinion of all those concerned, the chief event of the day was the annual supper of the Fifth Form Literary Society.

"Come along," cried Tinkleby, as the cheers which greeted a win for the Present were gradually dying away— "come along. I told Duster to have the grub ready at half-past five sharp, and it's a quarter to six."

"Shan't we get into a row for cutting tea?" asked Jack.

"No fear," answered the other. "Old Ward knows where we're going; and it's all right as long as we get back before lock-up."

The confectioner's shop patronized by the Melchester boys was situated in a quiet street some five minutes' walk from the school-gates. Why the proprietor's name should have been changed from Downing to "Duster" it would be difficult to say; but as long as his customers came furnished with ready money and good appetites, the probability is that the former would have been quite content to serve them under any nickname which they chose to invent.

At the back of "Duster's" establishment was a little square parlour, where boys repaired to eat ices and drink alarming quantities of Duster's famous home-made ginger-beer—a high explosive, which always sent the cork out with a bang, and to drink two bottles of which straight off would have been a risky business for any boy to attempt without first testing the staying power of his waistcoat-buttons, and putting several bags of sand in his jacket-pockets. In this parlour it was that the literary society assembled for their banquet; as many as could find room squeezing themselves on to the two short forms on either side of the table, and the remainder camping out wherever they could find room on the chairs, window-ledge, and a small sofa. At the close of a summer day the place was decidedly hot and stuffy, and the first thing everybody did was to pull off their coats and blazers and appear in their shirt-sleeves.

Tinkleby, as president, took the post of honour at the head of the table, and hammering the festive board with his fist, called on "Duster" to "bring in the grub and something to drink." To describe the banquet itself would need an abler pen than mine. The sausages were browned to perfection, the ices were pinker than a maiden's cheek, and the ginger-beer was stronger and more filling at the price than it had ever been before, and made those who drank it gasp for breath and feel as though they had swallowed a cyclone. James, surnamed "Guzzling Jimmy," distinguished himself by finishing up with ices, and then beginning all over again with cold ham and pickles; but at length, when even he had finished, there was a general hammering of the table, and a call for "speeches."

"Well, fire away," said the president. "Who's going to start?"

"I will," cried a boy named Dorris. "Gentlemen, I beg to propose a toast—success to the Fifth Form Literary Society, and with it I couple the name of our worthy president, Mr. Tinkleby; may he live long and be happy!"

This sentiment, though not very original, was received with great enthusiasm, the company showing their approval of it by administering to themselves fresh doses of "Duster's" liquid explosive.

The president, rising slowly to his feet, sticking his thumbs in the armholes of his waistcoat, and expanding that portion of his body which contained his supper, in imitation of the movements of Augustus Powler, Esq., M.P., cleared his throat, and began in pompous tones: "Mr. Mayor, ladies

74

and gentlemen, I cannot well express to you the delight with which I stand here to fulfil the pleasing duties which you have so kindly called upon me to perform. When I look round on the bright, young faces before me—"

The speaker paused to dodge a shower of crusts, corks, and other missiles; the owners of the "bright, young faces" evidently resented this personal allusion.

"Shut up, Tinky!" cried several voices. "Talk sense, can't you?"

The president smiled, and readjusted his nippers.

"I was about to remark," he continued in his natural tone, and with his accustomed fluency of speech, "I was about to remark that I thank you very much for having drunk my health. You were good enough to couple my name with that of our society. Gentlemen, I am convinced that the Fifth Form Literary Society has a great future before it. (Laughter.) I look forward to the time when we shall not grub here at 'Duster's,' but dine together in premises of our own. Our friend Mr. James has a nice little plot of ground in a soap-box, where he now grows mustard-and-cress, but which I have no doubt he would let to us on reasonable terms for building purposes. But, perhaps, I am looking a little too far ahead. As regards our immediate future, I intend making a determined effort to publish another number of the 'Portfolio.' (Cheers.) Mr. Ward has intimated his willingness to contribute a large number of Latin lines written by members of his class; while Mr. Sam Jones, the boot-cleaner, has offered to place his talented brush at our disposal, and produce a grand New-Year's Illustrated Supplement, entitled, 'Christmas in the Coal-Hole.' Gentlemen, I fear I am trespassing on your time and good nature. Mr. James, I see, is anxious to drink another toast. Once more I thank you for having drunk my health, and would now call upon you to drink that of Mr. Preston, who distinguished himself this afternoon by taking no less than seven of the old boys' wickets."

Great applause greeted the finish of the president's speech, and Preston's health was drunk amid a scene of the wildest enthusiasm. Cries of "On your pins, Preston!"—"Well bowled, sir!"—"Order!"—"Speak up!" etc., rent the air; while the pounding of fists and drumming of feet were continued until a game leg of one of the forms suddenly gave way, causing a temporary disappearance of half the company beneath the table.

Preston might have been able to howl, but he certainly could not talk, and it was hard for him to follow such a glib speaker as the president. However, the fact remained that he had distinguished himself, and brought honour to the Fifth Form in general by taking seven wickets; and for this reason his comrades would have been content had he merely stood up and reeled off the list of prepositions which govern the accusative, or quoted selections from the multiplication table. As it was, they awarded him a cordial reception, and filled up the pauses in his disjointed utterances with tumultuous applause.

"I'm much obliged to you fellows for drinking my health," began the bowler. "It's jolly good of you, and—all that sort of thing. (Cheers.) I did manage to bag seven wickets." (Renewed applause, interrupted by a warning shout of "Look out! this form's going again!") "I was going to say," continued the speaker, attempting to hide his embarrassment by pretending to drink out of an empty glass, "that it was rather a fluke—" (Shouts of "No! no!" "More pop for the gentleman!" and fresh outbursts of cheering.) "Well, I did the best I could, and—well—glad you're pleased, and all that sort of thing. (Alarums and excursions.) I suppose I ought to say something about this society, but, as regards that matter, the former speaker has rather taken the sails out of my wind. (Cheers and laughter.) No, I should say the *whales* out of my— (Yells of laughter.) Any way," concluded Preston, shouting to be heard above the general uproar, "I'm much obliged to you, and—all that sort of thing—"

It was not until several ginger-beer bottles had rolled off the table, and the rickety form had once more gone down with every soul on board, that a sufficient amount of order was restored to enable the president to call on somebody for a song.

"Sing yourself, Tinkleby," was the answer. "Give us 'Little Brown Jug.'"

The president complied with the request. Mead, a musical companion, ground out an unearthly accompaniment on "Duster's" little, broken-winded harmonium; and the company shrieked the chorus, regardless of time, tune, or anything but the earnest desire of each individual to make more noise than any one else.

When this deafening uproar had at length subsided, everybody was forced to remain quiet for a few moments to regain their breath. "Now, then," said Tinkleby, "who's next? What's that? All right. Bos. Jones says he will give us a recitation."

The announcement was received with a groan. Mr. Boswell-Jones was rather a pompous young gentleman, who expended most of his energies trying to live up to his double surname, and in consequence was not very popular with his schoolfellows. He rather fancied himself as an elocutionist; and though he might have seen "rocks ahead" in the manner in which the audience received the president's announcement, Boswell-Jones had sufficient confidence in his own powers to be blind to any lack of appreciation on the part of other people. He stood up and adjusted his necktie, cleared his throat, and began,—
"I remembah, I remembah,
The house where I was bawn,

("Euh! re—ah—lly!" murmured the listeners.)

The leetle window where the sun
Came peeping in at mawn."

"Whose little son?" interrupted Dorris.

"Shut up!" cried the president.

"Well, I only wanted to know," said Dorris in an injured tone. "I should call it jolly good cheek of anybody's son to come peeping in through my bedroom window—"

"Shut *up*!" exclaimed Tinkleby. "Go on, Bos."

"He never came a wink too soon,
Nor brought too long a day;
But now"—

continued the reciter with a great amount of pathos,

—"I often wish the night
Had bawn my breath away!"

"So do I," mumbled Paterson. "Let's have another song."

"I remembah, I remembah,
The roses, red and white—"

"Go on, Bossy," ejaculated the irrepressible Dorris; "you don't remember it at all, you're simply making it up as you go along."

A general disturbance followed this last interruption— the audience laughed, the president vainly endeavoured to restore order, and Boswell-Jones sat down in a rage, and refused to continue his oration.

"A song, a song!" cried several voices. "Jack Fenleigh, you know something; come on, let's have it."

Jack had a good voice, and with Mead extracting fearful groans and growls out of the harmonium, he started off on the first verse of "The Mermaid," a song which he was destined in after years to sing under strangely different circumstances:—

"Oh, 'twas in the broad Atlantic, 'mid the equinoctial gales,
That a gay young tar fell overboard, among the sharks and

whales;
And down he went like a streak of light, so quickly down
went                                                       he,
Until he came to a mermaid at the bottom of the deep blue
sea."

     Then the audience took up the chorus, and yelled,—
"Rule, Britannia! Bri—tann—ia rules the waves!
And Bri—tons never, never, ne—ver shall be
Mar—ri—ed to a mer—mai—ed
At the bottom of the deep blue sea!"

     The song was received with great enthusiasm, and the
performers might have been kept repeating the last chorus
until break of day on the following morning, it Tinkleby had
not suddenly jumped up, crying, "I say, you chaps, it's five-
and-twenty past seven. We shall be late for lock-up."

     Every one sprang to his feet. Dorris was the first to
reach the door, and being of a playful disposition caught up
a bundle of coats and blazers and bolted with them under
his arm. A moment later certain of the peaceful citizens of
Melchester were astonished at the sight of a dozen or more
young gentlemen tearing madly down the street in their shirt-
sleeves. And so ended the third annual supper of the Fifth
Form Literary Society.

# CHAPTER IX.

## "GUARD TURN OUT!"

"He felt for them as he had never felt for any other bird in the world. He was not envious ... but wished to be as lovely as they."—*The Ugly Duckling.*

"It is jolly to be here at Brenlands again," said Jack, as he sat dangling his legs from the kitchen table, and munching one of the sweet pods of the peas which his aunt was shelling. "I've been looking forward to it ever since last summer."

"Yes, and a pretty fuss I had to get you to accept my first invitation," answered Queen Mab; "I thought you were never going to condescend to favour us with your company. However, I've got you all here again, and it *is* jolly; and what's more, you managed to turn up at the proper time yesterday instead of coming half a day late, as you did last year, you rascal!"

The boy laughed. "Oh, well! you may put that down to Val," he answered. "He's quite taken me in hand lately, and has been in an awful funk for fear I should get into another row just before the holidays. You know those penny toys you get with a little thing like a pair of bellows under them that squeaks—well, I got a bird the other day and pulled off the stand, and stuck it in my shoe so that I could make a noise with it when I walked. Whenever I moved about in class, old Ward used to beseech me with tears in his eyes to wear another pair of boots. I used to come squeaking into assemblies a bit late on purpose, and send all the fellows into fits. It was a fearful joke; but poor old Val got quite huffy about it, and kept saying I should be found out, and that there was no sense in my 'monkey tricks,' as he called them."

"So they are," answered Queen Mab, smiling in spite of herself. "I should have thought you were old enough to find some more sensible amusement than putting pieces of penny toys in your boots. You may laugh at Valentine if you like, but I can tell you this, he's very fond of you, and that's the reason why he doesn't like to see you in trouble."

"I know he is," returned the boy briskly. "He's a brick; and I like him better than any other chap in the school."

Queen Mab went on shelling her peas, and Jack remained perched on the end of the table, quite content to continue watching her nimble fingers and sweet, restful face. It certainly was jolly to be back again at Brenlands. He was no longer the ugly duckling; Helen and Barbara were like sisters, and he got on with them swimmingly; all kinds of splendid projects were on the carpet, and there were plenty of long summer days to look forward to in which to carry them out. To be a careless dog of a schoolboy, ready for anything in the way of larks and excitement, and paying precious little attention to one's books or conduct record, might be a fascinating sort of existence; yet somehow it was not altogether unpleasant, once in a way, to become for a time a member of a more civilized and refined society, where gentler treatment encouraged gentler manners, where hearts were thought of as well as heads, where there was no black list, and where no one would have made a boast of being on it, had such a thing existed.

This year the mimic war operations were of a more advanced kind than had ever been attempted before. A fortress built of clay and pebbles was mined and blown up; and there still being some powder left, Jack successfully performed the feat of blowing himself up, and in doing so sustained the loss of an eyebrow. In order that this catastrophe should not alarm Queen Mab, the missing hair was replaced by burnt cork; but Jack, forgetting what had happened, sponged his face and rushed down to tea, where Barbara, after regarding him for a few moments in silence, leaned across the table and remarked, with a wise shake of her head, "Yes, I see—you've been shaving."

But what proved a source of endless delight to the two boys was an old, military bell-tent which Queen Mab had bought for their special use and amusement. They pitched it on a corner of the lawn, and were always repairing thither to read, and talk, and hold councils of war. It was delightful to speculate as to what doughty warriors might have been sheltered beneath it; and to imagine that sundry small rents and patches must be the result of the enemy's fire, and not due to the wear and tear of ordinary encampments.

Not satisfied with living in it by day, they determined to pass a night there also, and would not rest content until their aunt had given them permission to try the experiment.

"All we want," said Valentine, "is a mackintosh to spread on the ground, and a few rugs and sofa cushions, and a candle and a box of matches."

"Very well, you can have plenty of those," answered Queen Mab; "perhaps some day you won't be so well off, Valentine."

She spoke lightly enough, and with no foreshadowing of a visionary picture, often to haunt her mind in the days to come, of men lying silently under a clear, starlit sky, with belts on, rifles by their sides, and bayonets ready fixed.

The two boys prepared to put their project into immediate execution; and in connection with this their first but by no means last experience of a night under canvas, they were destined to fall in with a little adventure which must be recorded.

Shortly before the commencement of the holidays a lot of strawberries had been stolen from the garden, and Queen Mab feared lest a similar fate should overtake a fine show of pears which were just getting ripe.

"Well, good-night," she said, as she prepared to close the door on the two adventurers; "if you're cold, and want to come in, throw some pebbles up at my window."

"Oh, we shan't want to come in," answered Jack stoutly. "If you hear any one coming to steal the fruit, you shout, 'Guard turn out!' and we'll nab 'em."

The boys settled down like old campaigners. "Awful joke, isn't it?" said Jack.

"Yes, prime!" answered Valentine; "soldiering must be jolly."

Half an hour passed.

"I say," murmured Valentine, "this ground seems precious hard!"

"Yes," answered his companion. "I've tried lying on it every way, and I believe my bones are coming through my skin."

A long pause, and then, "I say, don't you think it's nearly morning?"

"Oh, no! the church clock has only just struck one."

The darkness seemed to lengthen out into that of a polar winter instead of a single night. At length the canvas walls began to grow grey with dawn, and Jack awoke with a shiver, wondering whether he had really been asleep or not.

"It's beastly cold," he muttered.

"Yes," answered Valentine. "I thought it was never going to get light. Look here, I'm determined I *will* sleep! What's the good of my being a soldier if I can't sleep in a tent?"

He turned over on his face, and had just dropped off into a doze, when he was awakened by Jack, who had reached over and was shaking his arm.

"I say—Val—who was that?"

"Who's what?" was the drowsy answer.

"Why! didn't you hear? Some one just walked down the path. It can't be Jakes; it isn't five o'clock."

Valentine rubbed his eyes, thought for a moment, and then suddenly sat up broad awake.

"The pears!" he whispered.

Both boys sprang up, unlaced the door of the tent, and sallied forth in the direction of the fruit garden.

"Don't make a row; walk on the grass border. Hist! there he is!"

There he was, sure enough; a boy about their own age, calmly picking pears and dropping them into a basket. Jack and Valentine slowly crept down by the side of the raspberry bushes, like Indians on a war-trail.

"Now then!" murmured the former, "charge!"

The thief jumped as if a gun had been fired off behind him, and started to run, but before he could reach the path he was fairly collared. He struggled violently, and then commenced to kick, whereupon his arm was suddenly twisted behind his back, a style of putting on the curb-rein with which fractious small boys will be well acquainted.

"Woa! steady now, 'oss!" said Jack facetiously. "Keep your feet quiet, or I shall put the screw on a bit tighter. Now then, what shall we do with him?"

"Put him into the tool shed," answered Valentine.

The culprit, finding himself fairly mastered, became more docile. His captors, however, turned a deaf ear to his pleadings to be let go; and thrusting him into the little outhouse, turned the key in the lock, and then began to wonder what they should do next.

"Well," said Jack, "we've got a prisoner of war now, and no mistake. What shall we do with the beggar? go for a policeman?"

"No, we don't want to get the chap sent to prison."

"If we tell Aunt Mab she'll let him go, and he ought to be punished."

"Of course he does—young villain! It's like his cheek coming here and bagging all the fruit."

"I have it!" said Jack, suddenly struck with a bright idea. "We'll lick him!"

Valentine hesitated. "I don't like setting on a chap two against one," he answered. "I don't mind a stand-up fight."

"Well, that's what I mean," answered Jack joyously. "Look here!" he continued, hammering on the door of the shed—"look here, you inside there! I'm going to punch your head for stealing those pears. If you like to come out I'll fight you, and then you can go; if not, you can stay where you are. Will you come?"

"Yes," answered the prisoner sullenly.

Twenty years ago a fight was not quite such a rare occurrence at Melchester School as it would be to-day. Jack threw off his coat with alacrity.

"Now, Val, you watch; and if the beggar tries to bolt, you leg him down."

With a dogged look the stranger took up his ground, and on the signal being given for the commencement of hostilities, lowered his head, and made a wild rush at his antagonist. The latter stepped aside, and greeted him with a smart cuff on the side of the head. Once more the visitor came on like a runaway windmill, but this time Jack walked backward and refused the encounter.

"Oh, look here," he cried, in an injured tone, "can't you do any better than that? Can't you stand up and hit straight? Don't you know how to box?"

"No."

"Well, what's the good of saying you'll come out and fight? What's your name?"

"Joe Crouch."

"Well then, Joseph, you'd better take your hook. There's your old basket, only just leave those pears behind; and don't come here again, or we'll set the bobby on your track."

Crouch marched off, evidently astonished at finding himself at liberty to depart. When he reached the gate, he turned, and touched his cap. "Morning, gen'lemen," he said, and so disappeared. Valentine laughed, and regarded his cousin with a queer look in his face.

"You are a rum fellow, Jack; you're always wanting to fight somebody. When you get two fellows against you like Garston and Rosher, you go at it like a tiger; and then another time, just because you get hold of a chap who can't knock you down, you back out and make peace."

"Well," answered the other, "there's no sport in licking a chap like that. I'll tell you what, I'm frightfully hungry."

The two adventurers had plenty to tell at breakfast that morning, and the interest in their capture lasted throughout the day. In the evening the young folks went out a favourite walk through the lanes and fields. Valentine and Barbara were running races on the way home; but Jack lingered behind with Helen, who was gathering ferns.

"Let me carry your basket," he said.

"Oh, don't you trouble; you'd rather run on with Val and Barbara."

"I expect you don't want me. I know you think I've got no manners, and in that you're about right."

"No, I don't think anything of the kind," said Helen, laughing. "I shall be very glad if you will carry the basket, because I want to talk to you."

"Now for a lecture," said Jack to himself.—"All right, fire away!"

"Well," began the girl, looking round at him with a twinkle in her eye, "I want to know why you didn't set Val on to fight that boy this morning, instead of offering to do it yourself."

"Oh, I don't know! It was my own idea; besides, I'm bigger and stronger."

"You mean you did it so that Val shouldn't get hurt, in the same way that you grappled with those three fellows who were ill-treating him at school."

"Pooh! he didn't tell you that, did he? He always lets you know all the bothers I get into. You'll think I do nothing but fight and kick up rows; and," added the speaker, with a pathetic look of injured innocence, "I've been behaving jolly well lately."

"I think you're a dear, good fellow for defending Val," said Helen warmly, "and I've been wanting to thank you ever since."

"It was nothing. 'Twasn't half as much as he did for me when he climbed that tree and freed my bootlace. I wish he wouldn't go telling you everything that happens at school."

"You were saying a day or so ago," said the girl, slyly, "that you didn't care for anybody, or for what people thought of you."

"Yes, I do," answered the ugly duckling; "I care a lot what you folks think of me at Brenlands."

"Why?"

"Why, because you're all better than I am, and yet you never try to make me feel it; but I do all the same. And I love you three and Queen Mab; and I love the place; and I should like to live here always. But outside of that," he added quickly, "I don't care a button for anything."

"I wish you wouldn't talk like that."

"But it's a fact."

"You mean," she answered gently, "that you've said it so often that at last you're beginning to believe it's true."

A few mornings later, when the boys came down to breakfast, they were surprised, on looking out of the window, to see no less a personage than Joe Crouch weeding the garden path.

"I found he was out of work, and his parents wretchedly poor," said Queen Mab; "so I said he might come and help Jakes by doing a few odd jobs. You know the old maxim," she added, smiling—"the beet way to subdue an enemy is to turn him into a friend."

The two boys took considerable interest in Crouch, regarding him as their own particular protégé. Joe, for his part, seemed to remember their early morning encounter with gratitude, as having been the means of landing him in his present situation. He had apparently a great amount of respect for Jack, and seeing the latter cutting sticks with a blunt knife, asked leave to take it home with him, and brought it back next day with the blades shining like silver, and as sharp as razors.

One afternoon, when the boys were lying reading in the tent, Barbara suddenly appeared in the open doorway, and stamping her foot, cried, "*Bother!*"

"What's up with you, Bar?"

"Why, that wretched Raymond Fosberton is in the house talking to Aunt Mab. He's walked over from Grenford; and he is going to stay the night."

Valentine groaned, and Jack administered a kick to an unoffending camp-stool.

"What does he want to come here for, I wonder?" continued Barbara. "Silly monkey! you should just see him in his white waistcoat and shiny boots—faugh!" And she choked with wrath.

Raymond's presence certainly did not contribute very much to the happiness of the party. He monopolized the conversation at tea-time, was very high and mighty in his manner, and patronized everybody in turn. He lost his temper playing croquet, and broke one of the mallets; and later on in the evening he cheated at "word-making," and because he failed to win, pronounced it a "stupid game, only fit for kids."

In Barbara, however, he found his match. She cared not two straws for all the Fosbertons alive or dead; and when the visitor, who had been teasing her for some time, went so far as to pull her hair, she promptly dealt him a vigorous box on the ear, a proceeding which so delighted the warlike Jack that he chuckled till bed-time.

Every one felt relieved when it came to tea-time on the following day. Raymond had announced his intention of walking home in the cool of the evening, and Queen Mab proposed that his cousins should accompany him part of the way.

They had walked about a mile, Jack and Helen being a little in advance of the others, when the girl caught hold of her cousin's arm.

"Oh, look!" she said, "there's a man coming who's drunk."

"Never mind," answered Jack stoutly; "he won't interfere with us."

The man, who had reeled into the hedge, suddenly staggered back into the middle of the road, and stood there barring the way.

"'Ello! Misser Fenleigh," he began, "'ow're you to-night, sir?"

Jack stared at the speaker in astonishment, and then recognized him as the same man who had spoken to them in Melchester.

"Look here!" he said hotly. "I've told you twice I don't know you. You just stand clear and let us pass."

By this time the remainder of the party had come up.

"Why, 'ere's Misser Fosbe'ton," continued the man, with a tipsy leer. "Now I jus' ask you, sir, if these two gen'lemen don't owe me some money for a drink."

Raymond's face flushed crimson, and then turned white.

"You've had too much already, Hanks," he said sharply; "just shut up, and stand out of the road."

"Oh, no offence!" muttered the man, staggering aside to let the cousins pass; "'nother time'll do jus' the same."

"Look here, Raymond, who is that fellow?" asked Valentine, as soon as they had got out of earshot of the stranger, "Twice he's come up to us in the street at Melchester, saying he knows us, and wanting money; and the last time, old Westford saw us talking to him, and we got into a beastly row, and were gated for a fortnight. Who is he?"

"Oh, he's a lazy blackguard called Ned Hanks; he's always poaching and getting drunk. He never does any work, except now and then he collects rags and bones, and sells them in Melchester."

"How does he know you?"

"He lives close to Grenford, and every one knows me there."

"But how does he know *us?*"

"I can't say. Haven't you ever seen him at Brenlands?"

"No, never."

"Well, I suppose he must have found out your name somehow; and he's always cadging for money for a drink. Don't you trouble to come any further. By-the-bye, next year I'm going to set up in diggings at Melchester. I shall be articled to a solicitor there; and if you fellows are still at the school, we might go out together."

"Confound that man!" said Jack, on the following morning; "I should like to find out who he is, and why he always speaks to us. I wonder if Crouch knows anything about him."

Joe Crouch was questioned, and admitted that he knew the man Hanks well by sight, and had sometimes spoken to him.

Jack explained the reason of his inquiry. "The fellow's got us into one row already. Why should he always be bothering us for money?"

Joe Crouch stood thoughtfully scratching his head for a moment with the point of the grass clippers.

"I dunno, sir," he answered; "but maybe I might find out."

# CHAPTER X.

## "STORMS IN A TEA-CUP."

"'Are you not in a warm room, and in society from which you may learn something? But you are a chatterer, and your company is not very agreeable.'"—*The Ugly Duckling.*

At the commencement of the winter term, in addition to being in the same class and dormitory, the two cousins were thrown still more together by occupying adjoining desks in the big schoolroom.

"Now I shall be able to keep an eye on you," said Valentine, "and see that you do some work."

"Shall you?"

"Yes; Helen gave me special instructions that I was to make you behave yourself. This is my last year; and the guv'nor says if I do well I shall go on then to an army coach to work up for Sandhurst."

"Well, I suppose I must behave myself, if it's Helen's orders," said Jack, laughing. "I wish I knew what I was going to do when I leave this place. I only wish I was going into the army like you. Some fine day I think I shall enlist."

"Oh, no, you wouldn't. What d'you think Queen Mab would say when she heard about it?"

"But she wouldn't hear about it," returned the other, with a touch of his restless discontent. "No one would hear about it. I should call myself Jones, or something of that sort. It would be a happier life than that I live at home; and what the guv'nor thinks he's going to do with me, I'm sure I don't know."

Valentine certainly did his best to follow out his sister's instructions, and keep Master Jack out of hot water. The latter seemed to have become a trifle more tractable; perhaps, finding other people were interested in him, he was

91

led to take more interest in himself. At all events, his conduct underwent a considerable change for the better, and his name no longer appeared on every page of the defaulters' book.

Football was now on, a sport which he specially enjoyed. In addition to this, Garston and Teal had left, and Rosher, who had now joined the Fifth, seemed to be increasing in wisdom as well as in stature, and no longer sought the bubble reputation in official visits to the headmaster's study. In short, Jack had improved with his surroundings. He and Valentine, in addition to their fretwork, had taken up carpentry; and on wet afternoons, when idle hands were steeped in mischief, they were always to be found in the shed which had been set apart for the boys to use as a sort of workshop. As far as the Fifth Form was concerned, only one incident happened to relieve the monotony of a somewhat uneventful term; and as one of our heroes was largely responsible for what took place, an account of the episode may as well be included in our story.

Jack, it should be said, was not to blame for what happened in the first place, his and Preston's share in the business was, as it were, only the effect arising from a primary cause; and for this, the real root of the matter, Tinkleby was solely responsible.

"Look here," said Tinkleby, "those fellows in the Sixth are running that debating show of theirs, and they get let off 'prep.' every Saturday night; wherefore I vote we join."

"They wouldn't have us," answered Dorris; "they won't allow any one to join if they are lower in the school than Sixth or Remove."

"Ah!" answered Tinkleby, adjusting his nippers, "but, don't you see, I should do it in this way—I should propose that our society be amalgamated with theirs."

"What society?" asked Preston the bowler.

"Why, the Fifth Form Literary Society, you blockhead!"

Preston and Dorris both exploded.

"You seem to think," continued Tinkleby, with a cynical smile, "that the only use for our society is to provide us with an excuse for having a feed once a year at 'Duster's;' but let me remind you, sir, that its main object, according to the original rules, was the cultivation of a taste for literary pursuits among its members."

"Yes," added Dorris, "and so you want to get off Saturday 'prep.' Fire away, Tinky, I'm with you."

That very afternoon Tinkleby addressed a large, square envelope to

*S. R. HENINGSON, Esq., Hon. Sec. Melchester School Debating Society.*

and having sealed it with an old military button, dropped it into the letter-box, a proceeding more in keeping with the importance of the communication than if he had delivered it by hand. The honorary secretary went one higher—he sent his reply by post. It was polite, and to the point. The committee of the debating society did not see their way to extend the limit of the rule relating to membership. They would be pleased to admit any of the Fifth Form who could obtain permission to attend the meetings, but they would not be entitled to vote, or to take any active part in the proceedings.

Tinkleby was incensed at this cool reception of his proposal, and harangued his comrades during a temporary absence of Mr. Ward from the classroom.

"They think such a confounded lot of themselves, with their miserable essays and dry debates. I'll bet we could stand up and spout as well as they can, on any subject you like to mention, from cribbing to astronomy."

"Of course we could," answered Boswell-Jones, who had prepared a paper entitled, "An Hour with the Poets," into which he had introduced all his favourite recitations, and which he longed to fire off at something in the shape of an audience—"of course we could; it's all that conceited beast Heningson. He thinks he's an orator—great ass!"

"Well, look here," said Tinkleby, fixing his nippers with an air of resolution and defiance, "Heningson's going to open a debate next Saturday. The subject is: 'That this house is of opinion that the moral and physical condition of mankind is in a state of retrogression.' We'll go and hear it. Ward'll let us do our 'prep.' in the afternoon. I've got a little plan in my head, and we'll take a rise out of these gentlemen."

The Melchester School Debating Society, as we have already mentioned, was established for the benefit of the senior boys, who held their meetings every Saturday night during the winter and Easter terms in what was known as the drawing classroom. It was conducted in a very solemn and serious manner. Redbrook, the head of the school, took the chair; while on the table before him, as a sign of his office and authority, a small hand-bell was placed, which he was supposed to ring when, in the heat and excitement of debate, members so far forgot themselves as to need a gentle reminder of the rule relating to silence. As a matter of fact, the chairman seldom, if ever, had any need to use this instrument, though on one occasion some wag removed it before the proceedings commenced, and substituted in its place the huge railway-bell used by Mullins, the school-porter; a jest which greatly incensed the grave and dignified assembly on whom it was practised. There was a proper mahogany ballot-box. The subjects for discussion always began, "That this house, etc.," and the secretary entered in a book exhaustive minutes of every meeting, which the chairman signed with a quill pen. These details are given in order that the reader may understand the character of the society in question, and be therefore in a better position to pass judgment on the outrageous behaviour of certain gentlemen whose conduct will shortly be described.

On the following Saturday evening, in answer to the formal invitation which they had received, Tinkleby and his friends filed into the room, looking very good and demure, and occupied the desk against the end wall, which they entered as though it had been a pew in church. The usual preliminaries were gone through, and the chairman called on "our worthy friend the secretary" to open the debate by moving, "That this house is of opinion that the moral and physical condition of mankind is in a state of retrogression."

For a time all went well. The visitors sat as mute as mummies, and the opener sought to justify his proposition by launching out into an impassioned discourse, which seemed rather inclined to resolve itself into a brief history of the world, and which the critical Tinkleby afterwards described as containing "more wind than argument." Touching briefly on the statements of the Hebrew chroniclers, Heningson proceeded with a wordy exposition of the manners and customs of ancient Greece, and from this stumbled rather abruptly into the rise of the Roman empire. Drawing a fancy and perhaps rather flattering portrait of one of the world-conquering legionaries, the speaker thought fit to compare it with that of a latter-day Italian organ-grinder who often visited the school, and who had recently been had up for being drunk and disorderly in the streets of Melchester.

"Gentlemen," exclaimed the orator earnestly, pointing accidentally at the chairman, but meaning to indicate the unfortunate musician, "is *this* the culmination of a race of gods? this inebriate, undersized—"

At this point the discourse was suddenly interrupted by a loud and prolonged snore. Heningson hesitated, and glanced up from his notes with a look of annoyance. He was about to proceed when a chorus of snores in every imaginable pitch and key effectively checked his utterance. With an indignant "Sh—s-h!" the audience turned in their seats to witness the following astonishing spectacle. At the back of the room every one of the half-dozen visitors sat, or rather sprawled, with his head upon the desk, in an attitude suggestive of the soundest slumber; the only variation in position being on the part of Jack Fenleigh, who lay back with a handkerchief thrown over his face like an old gentleman taking his after-dinner nap. The nasal concert continued, and the chairman smote his hand-bell.

"Firs' bell," murmured Tinkleby drowsily, "stop working;" while Dorris became suddenly afflicted with a catch in his breath which caused a succession of terrific snorts, each of which nearly cracked the windows.

"Here, stop that noise!" cried Redbrook, springing to his feet in great wrath. "Wake 'em up, somebody!"

An obliging member caught Tinkleby by the arm, and gave him a prodigious shake.

"Shur up," growled that gentleman. "Give me back my pillow, 'tisn't time to ger up. Hallo! have I been asleep? I'm beastly sorry."

One by one the other occupants of the visitors' gallery were made to understand that they were not in their beds. Jack Fenleigh, however, absolutely refused to return from the land of dreams. He was shaken, pinched, and pommelled, but all to no purpose; his snores only became louder, and the style more fantastic.

Meanwhile a heated altercation was going on between the chairman and the president of the Fifth Form Literary Society.

"Look here, Tinkleby, we don't want any more of your silly foolery, so just stop it."

"My dear sir, I'm doing nothing."

"Well, why did you begin?"

"If you mean my having dropped off to sleep, I'm very sorry; but really there's something in the air of the place—"

"Haw-r-r-r-ratch," interposed Jack Fenleigh. Redbrook rose from his chair, boiling with wrath.

"Just clear out!" he cried. "Go on—all the lot of you!" The visitors demurred, but being outnumbered three to one, they were seized and hustled unceremoniously out of the room. In the midst of all this commotion, however, Fenleigh J., still continued in an unbroken slumber, and was distinctly heard snoring louder than ever as his companions dragged him off down the passage.

Fifth Forms. Tinkleby and his comrades were designated a set of rowdy jackasses; and they replied to the compliment by declaring that a fraternity of live donkeys was better than a collection of stuffed owls, and advising Heningson to patent his discourse as an infallible cure for insomnia. Cutting allusions to the "Literary Society" and sarcastic retorts were exchanged in the corridors and playing-field; and so the feud continued.

All his classmates were charmed with Jack's share in the performance.

"You wait," was his invariable answer to their congratulations; "I'll take a better rise out of them before long."

For the time being this little joke gave rise to a rather strained relationship between the members of the Sixth and

For a time this boast was not considered to imply any definite intention on the speaker's part to play any further pranks on the members of the debating society; but at length a rumour got abroad that something *was* going to happen. Fenleigh J. and Preston had been seen more than once taking counsel together in out-of-the-way corners, and exchanging mysterious nods and winks.

"The visitors were seized, and hustled unceremoniously out of the room."

They were known to have spent the free time between "prep." and supper, on two consecutive evenings, alone together in the workshop, with the door locked. A great deal of hammering went on, but no one could find out what they were making. When questioned on the subject, they professed a lamb-like state of innocence; and even Tinkleby himself could give no explanation of their conduct. A fortnight after the delivery of Heningson's essay, the debating society held an important meeting, the announcement of which, posted the previous evening on the notice-board, was worded as follows:—

M. S. D. S.
*Saturday, November ...th.*
DEBATE.

"That this house approves of the settlement of all international disputes by arbitration instead of war,"

*Aff.,* Mr. N. J. CARTER.
*Neg.,* Mr. SHEPHERD.

The members turned up in force, for this time the openers of the discussion were the two leading lights of the society, and the contest between them was certain to prove an intellectual treat which ought not to be missed. Carter's style of oratory was of the impassioned order; he thumped on the desk, and went through the "extension motions," with the exception of that awful movement where you bend double and try to touch your toes. It was rumoured that he wrote deep, unintelligible poetry that did not rhyme; and if the school rules had not forbidden the practice, he would have worn long hair and a fly-away necktie. Shepherd, on the other hand, went in for logic, unadorned by any movements suggestive of setting-up drill. His style bore a suspicious resemblance to that of Augustus Powler, Esq., M.P. He stuck his thumbs in the armholes of his waistcoat, and pushed forward that portion of his body which it would have been unfair to strike at in a fight. It would be impossible to give here anything like a detailed report of the proceedings. From the moment when the chairman rose to introduce the first speaker, every one felt that the meeting would be one of unusual interest; and in one sense they were certainly destined not to be disappointed. Carter was in great form; he dealt the desk such terrific blows that the ink spurted out of the ink-pots, and ran down on to the secretary's breeches. War, he declared, was legalized murder, and the soldier little better than a hired assassin. Napoleon Bonaparte was far more roughly handled than at Leipsic or Waterloo; and a long list of conquerors, ranging back to Alexander the Great, were, figuratively speaking, torn from their graves and hung in chains. At length, having dwelt on the enormous cost of standing armies, and other more practical aspects of the subject, the speaker concluded with a vivid picture of the horrors of a battlefield, and was in the act of quoting a verse of poetry, when he was suddenly silenced by an unlooked-for interruption.

"The bursting shell, the gateway wrenched asunder,
The rattling musketry, the clashing blade;
And ever and anon, in tones of thunder,
The—"

Bang!
Every one started; something like a miniature representation of the "bursting shell" had just exploded in the neighbourhood of the blackboard. A boy sitting close by stooped down and picked up from the floor a small fragment of burnt tissue-paper.
"Who threw that?" he exclaimed.
"What is it?" asked the chairman.

"Why, one of those 'throw-downs.'"

Redbrook glanced round the room in angry astonishment.

"Look here," he said sharply, "I don't know who did it, but if any of you have come to play the fool, you'd better leave the room at once, for we aren't going to have any more nonsense like we had the other night."

The audience turned in their seats, and stared at one another in amazement. Most of my readers will probably have some practical knowledge of the small, round paper pellets known as "throw-downs," which explode when flung against anything; and it was difficult to imagine that any member of the select and decorous Melchester School Debating Society would cause an interruption by flinging such things about in the middle of an important discussion.

"Go on, Carter," said the chairman.

"Shan't!" returned the other, snappishly. "I've finished."

Shepherd was now called upon to open on the side of the negative.

"War," he began, assuming his accustomed attitude, and beaming round on his listeners with a very good imitation of the Powler smile—"war is like surgery. When drugs are of no avail, we are often forced to resort to the use of the knife, and so—"

Another mimic bomb exploded in the very centre of the speaker's waistcoat, causing him to jump nearly out of his skin. Redbrook sprang to his feet in a towering rage, and as he did so another projectile burst on the open pages of the minute book.

"Who threw those things? I will find out!"

A babel of voices rose in reply. No one had done it. The door was shut, the windows were fastened, a hasty search was made in the cupboards and under the back desks, in the hope of discovering a lurking enemy; but even while the search was in progress another missile went off under the secretary's chair.

101

"Who is it?" shouted Redbrook. "Where do they come from?"

"That seemed to fall from the ceiling," answered Heningson; "yes—look there!"

Above the hanging gas-jet in the centre of the room was an ornamental iron grating, between the apertures of which there now appeared about an inch and a half of brass tube, like the end of a big peashooter. A moment later there was a prodigious puff, and four "throw-downs" exploded with a simultaneous crash in the centre of the chairman's table.

"There's some one up on the roof!" cried several voices.—"Stop it, you villain!"

"How could any one get there?"

"There's a trap-door at the end of the passage," exclaimed Shepherd. "Quick! we shall cut him off."

A rush was made for the door, but it refused to open; some one had evidently blocked the exit from the outside, by placing a short form lengthways across the passage. The drawing classroom formed part of a one-storied building which bounded one side of the school quadrangle. Finding the door closed, Shepherd dashed to the nearest window, and flinging it open dropped out on to the gravel, an example which was speedily followed by the chairman and several members of the audience. Breathing out all manner of threats, they ran round through the nearest door and gained the entrance to the passage. The trap-door in the ceiling was wide open, and communicating with it was a curious, home-made ladder, consisting of an old post, with half a dozen rough cross pieces fastened to it with stout nails. A candle end was lying on the floor, and with its aid Shepherd climbed up and explored the roof; but the bird had flown.

After such an interruption it was no use attempting to continue the debate, and Redbrook and his companions spent the remainder of the evening trying to discover the authors of this outrage.

The culprits, however, had made good their escape; no one remembered having seen the ladder before, and it was impossible to say to whom it belonged. The members of the debating society were clearly outwitted; and not wishing to make the story of their discomfiture too public, they determined for the present to let the matter drop, at the same time announcing their intention of taking dire vengeance on any irreverent jokers who should rashly attempt to disturb their meetings in future. Two days later, Valentine was sitting at his desk reading, when he was joined by his cousin.

"I borrowed your brass ruler the other afternoon," said the latter, producing something from under his coat.

"Yes, I know all about it, you villain!"

"I only used it as a sort of pea-shooter."

"Oh, I've heard all about your little game; Preston told me."

Jack tried to look innocent, and then laughed.

"It's no use, Val, old chap, you'll never make a good boy of me. It's the old story of the silk purse and the sow's ear."

Valentine laughed too.

"I'm afraid I never shall," he answered. "The joke is that you're always ready to bring the whole place about your ears with some mad prank, and then when a cartload of bricks does fall on your head, you say, 'It's just your luck, and that—'"

"A collection will be taken at the door in aid of the poor fund at the close of the present service," interrupted the other. "Good-bye—I'm off!"

He moved away a step or two, then came softly back, and began to rumple his cousin's hair; whereupon an exciting struggle ensued, which brought them both down on to the floor, and ended with the edifying spectacle of the preacher sitting flushed and triumphant on the congregation's chest.

# CHAPTER XI.

## "OUT OF THE FRYING-PAN—"

"Above all, beware of the cat."— *The Ugly Duckling.*

"Here, Val, you're just the man I want! Tell me something to say."

It was a broiling afternoon. The summer term had once more come round, and Jack, with his coat off, was sitting in a shady corner of the schoolroom wrestling with a letter to Queen Mab.

"I write to her nearly every blessed week," he continued, "and the consequence is I've never got anything to say. I've told her how jolly it is to think that in four weeks' time we shall be at Brenlands again; and now I'm stuck, and I can't get any further."

"Have you told her how well you've been doing in cricket this season?"

"No."

"Well, I have; so it doesn't much matter. Look here! Raymond Fosberton's outside, and wants to see you."

"Oh, tell him to go to Bath!" answered Jack, making another stab at the ink-pot with his pen. "I want to finish this letter."

"No, come along," answered Valentine, laughing. "You must be civil to the fellow; he's been waiting about for nearly a quarter of an hour."

"Do him good," growled the scribe, reluctantly pitching his untidy epistle into a very disorderly desk. "He only comes here to show off. Just because he's in a lawyer's office, he thinks he's a big pot, and all he does is to write copies like a kid in the Lower School."

According to his own opinion, Raymond Fosberton had blossomed out into the full-blown man. He wore a light check suit of the very latest fashion, a rosebud adorned his button-hole, and he tapped the toe of his highly-polished, patent-leather boots with the point of a silver-mounted cane.

"Hallo!" he exclaimed; "what the dickens d'you want to keep a chap waiting so long for? I can tell you my time's more valuable than yours. Look here! I'm sorry I haven't been able to ask you boys to come and see me before, but nearly every night since I've been here I've been engaged. However, I want you to get leave to come and have tea at my rooms on Wednesday, and after that we'll go to the fair. You know what I mean. It's held once a year in a big field on the other side of the town; there are shows, and round-abouts, and all that sort of thing."

"Thanks," answered Valentine, "but I'm afraid we can't go."

"Why not?"

"Because the rule of the school is that no boys are allowed to go to Melchester Fair. Old Westford is awfully strict about it. Two years ago some fellows went, and had a row with one of the showmen, and it got into the papers."

"Oh, rubbish! you can say you're only going out to tea." Valentine shook his head.

"Oh, yes, you can," continued Raymond. "By-the-bye, there's a fellow here called Rosher, isn't there? My guv'nor knows his people, and told me to ask him out sometimes; tell him to come too, if he can."

"We can't do it," answered Valentine decisively; "while the fair's on, Westford won't even give fellows leave to go down into town."

"Nonsense!" answered Raymond contemptuously. "You leave it to me, and I'll manage it all right. Now I must cut back to the office. Ta! ta!"

On Wednesday afternoon the two cousins were preparing to start for the cricket field, when a small boy brought them word that the headmaster wished to see them for a moment in his study.

"What's the row now, I wonder?" said Jack. "'Pon my word, it's so long since I went to the old man's study that I feel quite nervous."

The interview was not of a distressing nature. "I have received a letter from your uncle," began Mr. Westford, "asking for you to be allowed to go and meet him at the station this afternoon at five o'clock. He wishes also to see Rosher, so you can tell him that he may go. Be back, of course, in time for supper."

"I wonder what brings Uncle Fosberton to Melchester," said Valentine to Jack as they walked away together.

"Can't say," returned the other. "I don't want to see him; but I suppose we must go. Let's hunt up Rosher."

A few minutes before five, the three boys entered the booking-office at the railway station.

"I wonder which platform it is!" said Jack. "Hallo! there's Raymond."

The gentleman in question came forward, flourishing his silver-mounted cane.

"Well, my dear nephews," he cried, laughing. "How are you to-day? Did old Westford get my letter all right?"

"What letter?" asked Valentine.

"Why, the letter asking for you to come out."

"But uncle wrote that!"

"Not a bit of it!" answered Raymond triumphantly. "I did it. I had a bit of the manor note-paper, and I sent it to our man to post it from Grenford. Ha! ha! I told you I'd manage the business!"

Rosher chuckled, Jack whistled, but Valentine remained silent.

"Look here, Raymond," said Valentine, after a moment's pause, "I tell you straight, I don't believe in this sort of thing. I'm going back."

"Don't be a fool, man," retorted the other. "You can't go back now, or they'll want to know the reason. Come along to my diggings and have some tea, and I'll bear all the blame."

With some reluctance Valentine agreed to go with the party to his cousin's lodgings. Raymond did not seem on very good terms with his landlady. The tea was a long time coming; and when at length it did make its appearance, the fare consisted only of bread and butter, and a half-empty pot of jam.

"Sorry I can't offer you anything more," remarked the host, "but just now I've run rather short of cash. Better luck next time."

As soon as the meal was over, Raymond repeated his proposal that they should visit the fair.

"It's an awful joke," he said. "I'm going, and you chaps may as well come along too."

"It's all very well for you to go," answered Jack, "but with us it's different. Any one can see by our hat-bands that we belong to the school; and if it gets to Westford's ears that we've been, we shall stand a jolly good chance of being expelled."

"Oh, well! if you're afraid, don't go," answered Raymond, with a sneer. "I thought you were a chap who didn't care for anything. Will you go, Rosher?"

"I don't mind."

"Come on, then; don't let's stick here all the evening."

The four boys put on their hats and sauntered out into the street. Valentine said good-night, and turned off in the direction of the school; but Jack lingered behind with the other two.

"That's right," said Raymond, taking his arm; "I knew you'd come."

The evening was always the gayest part of the day at Melchester Fair. Crowds of people from the town and surrounding neighbourhood jostled each other in the open spaces between the tents and booths, while the noise of bands, steam-organs, and yelling showmen was something terrific.

"I say, have either of you fellows got change for a sovereign?" asked Raymond. "You haven't? well, you pay, and I'll settle up with you some other time."

The boys wandered round the field, listening to the cheap Jacks, and the proprietors of various exhibitions, which were all "just a-goin' to begin." They patronized a shooting-gallery, where they fired down long tubes with little rifles, which made the marksman's hands very black, and seemed to carry round the corner. Jack, however, succeeded in hitting the bull's-eye, and ringing the bell, and was rewarded with a handful of nuts.

"Come on," said Rosher; "let's have a turn on the wooden horses," and the party accordingly moved off in the direction of the nearest round-about. The steeds were three abreast, and Raymond mounted the one on the outside. A little group of factory boys were standing close by, and, just as the engine started, one of them thought fit to enliven the proceedings with a joke.

"Hallo, mister! how much starch d'you put on your weskit?"

"That much!" answered Raymond, snappishly, and leaning outwards in passing he dealt the speaker a sharp cut with his cane.

"Yah! Thatches!" cried the boy, and every time the whirligig brought his assailant into view the shout was repeated.

In the year of grace 1877 some traces still remained of an ancient feud between the school and the boys of the town. The name "Thatches" had been invented by the latter on account of the peculiar pattern of straw hat worn by their adversaries; while the answering taunt always used in those warlike times was, "Hey, Johnny, where's your apron?" a remark which greatly incensed the small sons of toil, who usually wore this garment.

"What have you been doing to those chaps?" asked Jack, as the horses slowed down and the yell was repeated.

"One of them cheeked me, and I hit him with my stick."

"Well, we'd better slip away as soon as this thing stops; we don't want to have a row with them here."

Unfortunately for the three boys, their steeds stopped just opposite the hostile group. Jack pushed through them with an expression of lofty contempt, an example followed by Rosher; but Raymond was stupidly led into a further exchange of incivilities.

"Don't you give me any more of your confounded impudence, you miserable little cads, or I'll give you another taste of this stick."

The "cads" answered with a shout of derisive laughter, and a few more straggling clansmen joining the band, they followed after the three friends, keeping at a safe distance, and repeating their cries of "Yah! Thatches! Hit one yer own size!" and other remarks of a similar nature.

"We can't go on like this," said Jack. "They'll follow us all round the fair. Shall we charge the beggars?"

"No," answered Raymond. "Let's go into the circus, and that'll put them off the track. You fellows pay, and I'll owe it you; I don't want to change my sovereign here."

Rosher paid for three shilling seats, and the trio entered the big circular tent, thus for the time being effectually escaping from the pursuing band of unfriendly natives.

The performance had just commenced, and though the display was by no means brilliant, yet the boys enjoyed it, and soon forgot the existence of everything except clowns, acrobats, and trained horses.

"*I say!*" exclaimed Rosher suddenly, "d'you know what the time is? It's close on nine o'clock!"

"By jingo!" answered Jack, "we must do a bolt."

"No, don't go," interposed Raymond; "you can't get back in time now, so you may as well stay and see the end. If you'll come round by my lodgings, I'll get my guv'nor to write a letter of excuse."

"I don't want any more of your letters," murmured Jack, "it's too risky. We'd better hook it."

"No, stay; you can't get back in time now, so what's the good of losing part of the performance?"

After some further discussion, Jack and Rosher decided to remain, and so kept their seats until the end of the performance. It was quite dark when they emerged from the tent, and every part of the fair was lit up with flaring paraffin lamps. They had not gone very far when, as ill-luck would have it, a shrill cry of "Hallo! Thatches!" showed that they had been sighted by some small scout of the enemy.

"I've got some coppers left," said Rosher; "let's have a shot at the cocoa-nuts."

They stopped opposite a pitch, and began bowling at the fruit. The first two or three shies were unsuccessful; then Jack knocked down a nut.

"I'm not going to let you beat me!" cried Rosher. "Here; mister, give me some more balls."

A fresh group of town boys were hovering about in the rear, their number being now augmented by one or two of a larger size.

"Yah! Thatch! you can't hit 'em! Come 'ere and let's see that stick you was talking about."

"I say," whispered Raymond to his cousin, "wouldn't it be a lark to pretend to make a good shot, and knock that lamp over." He pointed as he spoke to one of the flaring oil lamps which, fastened to a stake a few feet above the ground, illuminated the line of nuts.

"No, don't do it," answered Jack; but the warning came too late. Raymond threw with all his might, and, as ill-luck would have it, the aim was only too true; the heavy wooden ball hit the lamp a sounding whack, dashed it from its stand, and the next moment the canvas screen at the back of the pitch against which it fell was all in a blaze.

In an instant all was confusion. Quick as thought Raymond turned, and slipped away between the wheels of a caravan which stood close by. The proprietor of the pitch sprang forward and seized Jack by the coat.

"'Ere, you did that," he cried, "and you did it a purpose."

The crowd of juvenile roughs closed in behind.

"Yes, 'e did it," they cried; "'e's the man."

"I didn't do it," retorted the boy. "Leave go!"

Rosher leaned forward, and giving his friend a nudge, uttered the one word,—

"*Bolt!*"

Jack's blood was up. He wrenched himself free of the man's grasp, and plunged into the little crowd of riff-raff, striking heavy blows to right and left. Rosher did the same; and the enemy, who were nothing but a pack of barking curs, went down like ninepins, falling over one another in their efforts to escape.

The two fugitives rushed on, stumbling over tent-ropes and dodging round the booths and stalls, until they came to the outskirts of the fair. Then they paused to take breath and consider what was to be done next. The glare of the burning canvas and a noise of distant shouting, which could be clearly distinguished above the other babel of sounds, showed the quarter from which they had come.

"Where's Raymond?" cried Jack.

"I don't know," answered Rosher; "we can't wait here, or we shall be collared."

"Didn't you see what became of him? I don't like the thought of leaving the fellow—"

The sentence was never finished; for at that moment two men suddenly appeared from behind a neighbouring stall. One was arrayed in a blue uniform with bright buttons, and his companion was at once recognized by the boys as being the proprietor of the cocoa-nut pitch.

"Here they are!" shouted the latter, catching hold of the policeman's arm; "now we've got 'em!"

Quick as thought the two schoolfellows turned and dashed off at the top of their speed. Beyond the outskirts of the fair all lay in darkness; a high hedge loomed in front of them. Jack scrambled up the bank, crashed through the thorn bushes, and fell heavily to the ground on the other side. In an instant he had regained his feet, and was running for his life with Rosher by his side. In this manner they crossed three fields, stumbling over uneven places in the ground, scratching their hands, and tearing their clothes in the hedges, and at length landed nearly up to their knees in a ditch half-full of mud and water.

"It's no good, Fenleigh, I can't go any further. I'm completely pumped."

Struggling on to a bit of rising ground, the fugitives halted and turned round to listen. The glare of light and noise of the fair had been left some distance behind them, and there were no sounds of pursuit. The night was very dark, and everything in their immediate neighbourhood was quiet and still.

"We must get to the town some other way," said Jack. "Doesn't the road to Hornalby pass somewhere here on the right?"

"I don't know," answered Rosher; "we ought to strike some road or other if we keep going in that direction."

The boys continued their flight, varying their walk by occasionally breaking into a jog-trot. At length they found themselves in a narrow lane; but after wandering down it for nearly half a mile, their further progress was barred by the appearance of a private gate.

"Here they are! now we've got them!"

"Botheration!" cried Jack, "we've come wrong; this leads to some farm. We shall never get home at this rate."

Retracing their steps the way they had come, the two unfortunate adventurers at length found themselves on the Hornalby road; but when they reached Melchester, and were hurrying down the side street past "Duster's" shop, the cathedral clock struck half-past eleven.

"Oh, my!" said Rosher; "how shall we get in? Everybody will be in bed. We shall have to knock up old Mullins at the lodge."

"No fear," answered Jack. "We must get into Westford's garden, and from there into the quad; then we'll try some of the windows."

The plan was carried out, and a few moments later the two boys were standing in the dark and deserted playground. Jack made a circuit of the buildings on tiptoe, and then returned to his companion.

"All the classroom windows are fast," he said, "but there's one on the first landing belonging to the bathroom that's open. What we must do is this. Under the bench in the workshop is that ladder thing that Preston and I made last year. We must fetch it, and you must hold it while I get up to the window. Then you must put the ladder back, and I'll creep down and let you in at the side door. The workshop's locked, but luckily I've got the key in my pocket!"

The scheme was successful, and ten minutes later the two wanderers were creeping up the main staircase. Rosher had a private bedroom; and Jack, moving softly, and undressing in the dark, managed to get into bed without awakening any of the other boys in his dormitory.

# CHAPTER XII.

## "—INTO THE FIRE."

"One of the little boys took up the tin soldier and threw him into the stove."—*The Brave Tin Soldier.*

"Hallo, Fenleigh! You were back precious late last night," said Walker, the Sixth Form boy in charge of the dormitory.

"Yes," answered the other carelessly. "I had leave to go out to tea."

The reply seemed to satisfy Walker; but there was one person in the room to whom Jack knew he would have to make a full confession. While dressing he avoided Valentine's questioning glances, but after breakfast he was forced to give his cousin a full account of all that had happened. A dark frown settled on the latter's face as he listened to the recital, which he several times interrupted with impatient ejaculations.

"I knew you'd be in a wax with me," concluded Jack, with an air of defiance; "but it can't be helped now. You'll never make a saint of me, Val, old chap, so don't let's quarrel."

"It's not you that I'm angry with," answered Valentine wrathfully, "it's that beast of a Raymond. It's just his way to get other people into a mess, and leave them to get out of it as best they can. I suppose he never paid up his share of the money you spent?"

"Not he. Never mind, we got out of the bother a lot better than I expected."

Valentine shook his head.

"I hope to goodness you won't be found out," he said anxiously. "If you are, you'll stand a jolly good chance of being expelled."

"Oh, we're safe enough. Don't you fret," answered Jack lightly.—"Hallo, Tinkleby, what's up with you?"

The president of the Fifth Form Literary Society was striding across the gravel, fingering his nippers, as he always did when excited.

"Haven't you heard?" he answered. "Some one's in for a thundering row, I can tell you."

"Why, what do you mean?"

"Why, Mullins says that some man from the fair came this morning, and wanted to see the headmaster. He says one of our fellows was up there last night, kicking up a fine shindy, and set his show on fire; and he means to find out who it is, and summon him for damages. Mullins told him he'd better call again later on, as Westford was at breakfast. My eye! I pity the chap who did it, if it's true, and he's collared."

The clang of the school bell ended the conversation, and Tinkleby rushed off to impart his news to other classmates.

The distressed look on Valentine's face deepened, but he said nothing.

"Pooh!" exclaimed Jack, sticking his hands in his pockets, and making the gravel fly with a vicious kick. "Let him come and say what he likes. What do I care?"

The school had reassembled after the usual interval, and the Sixth Form were sitting in their classroom waiting for the arrival of the headmaster. A quarter of an hour passed, and still he did not arrive. At length the door opened, and Mullins poked his head inside.

"Mr. Westford wants to see all those gentlemen who are in charge of the different dormitories—now, at once, in his study."

A murmur of surprise followed the announcement, as the boys indicated rose to their feet and prepared to obey the summons. On entering the study they found a shabby-looking man standing just inside the door, who eyed them all

117

narrowly as they came in. The headmaster sat at his writing-table looking stern and troubled. The twelve prefects arranged themselves in a semicircle, and stood silently waiting and wondering what could have happened.

"You say this took place about a quarter past ten?"

"Yes, sir," answered the man, twirling his hat with his fingers. "As near as I can say, it must have been about a quarter a'ter ten."

"I have sent for you," continued Mr. Westford, turning to the group of senior scholars, "to know if any of the boys were absent from any of the dormitories at the usual bed-time."

"One was absent from Number Five, sir," said Walker.

"Who?"

"Fenleigh J., sir."

"Why didn't you report him? What time did he return?"

"I don't know, sir. I was asleep when he came back. He said he'd had leave to go out to tea."

"Was any one else absent from any of the rooms? Very well. You may go. Redbrook, send Fenleigh J. to me at once."

A minute or so later the culprit entered the room.

"That's the young feller I want!" exclaimed the stranger. "I could tell him anywheres in a moment."

"Fenleigh, were you at the fair last night?"

"Yes, sir."

"What were you doing there? You know my orders?"

The boy was silent.

"I can tell you what he was doing," interrupted the man. "He knocked over one of my lamps and set my screen afire; and a'ter that he started fightin', and I was obliged to fetch a p'liceman. But there was two of 'em, this one and another."

"Did this really happen, Fenleigh?"

"Yes, sir."

"Who else was with you?"

"My cousin, Raymond Fosberton. It was he who knocked over the lamp."

"That's a lie!" interrupted the man. "It was you done it. I seed you with my own eyes."

"I don't think I need detain you any longer," said Mr. Westford, turning to the owner of the cocoa-nuts. "I need hardly say I regret that one of my scholars should be capable of such conduct. I shall make some further inquiries, and if you will call again this evening, whatever damage has been done shall be made good."

The man knuckled his forehead and withdrew. Jack was left alone with his judge, and felt that the case was ended.

"Now, sir," said the latter, in a cold, rasping tone, "you have succeeded in bringing public disgrace on the school, and I hope you are satisfied. Go to the little music-room, and remain there for the present."

There was something ominous in the brevity of this reprimand. No punishment had been mentioned, but in the school traditions the little music-room was looked upon as a sort of condemned cell. Every one knew the subsequent fate of boys who had been sent there on previous occasions; and in a short time the news was in everybody's mouth that Fenleigh J. was going to be expelled. It was a grave offence to hold any communication with a person undergoing solitary confinement, yet, before Jack had been very long a prisoner, a pebble hit the window, and looking out he saw Rosher.

"I say," began the latter dolefully, "I'm awfully sorry you've been found out. If you like, I'll go and tell Westford I was with you."

"Of course you won't. What's the good?"

"Well, I thought perhaps you'd think I was a sneak if I didn't. I'm afraid you'll get the sack," continued Rosher sadly. "It was awfully good of you, Fenleigh, not to split; you always were a brick. I say, we were rather chummy when you first came, if you remember; and then we had a bit of a row. I suppose it don't matter now. If you like, I'll write you when you get home."

It was something, at such an hour, to have the sympathy and friendship even of a scapegrace like Rosher. The prisoner said "it didn't matter," and so they parted.

For some time Jack wandered round the little room, swinging the blind cords, and trifling with the broken-down metronome on the mantelpiece. It was this very instrument that had been upset when he sent Rosher sprawling into the fireplace; and yet, here was the same fellow talking about keeping up a correspondence. A litter of torn music lay on the top of the piano; among it a tattered hymn-book. Jack turned over the pages until he came to "Hark, hark, my soul!" and then, sitting down, played the air through several times with one finger. It was a tune that had been popular on Sunday evenings at Brenlands, and the children had always called it Queen Mab's hymn.

Jack shut the book with a bang. In less than a fortnight's time he ought to have been with her again, and what would she think of him now?

Dinner was over in the big hall, and most of the boys had started for the playing-field. Mr. Ward sat correcting exercises in the deserted Fifth Form classroom, when there was a knock at the door, and Valentine entered.

"Well, Fenleigh," said the master kindly, "what do you want?"

"I came to speak to you, sir, about my cousin Jack. Don't you think there's any chance of getting Mr. Westford to let him off?"

"I'm afraid there isn't. I don't see what excuse can be offered for your cousin's conduct."

"But there is an excuse, sir," persisted Valentine, his love of honour and justice causing the blood to mount to his cheeks at the recollection of Raymond Fosberton's share in the adventure. "It was not all Jack's fault, and it'll be an awful shame if he's expelled."

Had it been another fellow, Mr. Ward might have pooh-poohed the objection, and sent the speaker about his business; for, it being nearly the end of the term, the master had plenty of work to occupy his attention. He was not given to making favourites among his pupils, but Valentine was a boy who had won his respect; and so he laid down his pen to continue the conversation.

"I still fail to see what can be said on your cousin's behalf. If it was not his fault, who then is to blame?"

Valentine hastily recounted all that had happened on the previous afternoon. He did not hesitate to give a true account of the bogus invitation, and repeated all that Jack had told him as to what had taken place at the fair. Mr. Ward listened patiently till he had heard the whole of the story.

"There certainly is something in what you say," he remarked. "But the fact remains that your cousin went to the fair in defiance of the school rules. There was no reason at all why he should have gone. You say you came back; then why couldn't he have done the same?"

"If I'd thought that my staying away would have made it any the worse for him, I'd have gone to the fair myself," said Valentine desperately.

Mr. Ward smiled.

"Well, what do you want me to do?" he asked. "I don't see that I can be of much service to you in the matter. The only thing I can advise you to do is to go to Mr. Westford, and tell him exactly what you have told me."

"I thought perhaps you might say a word for him too, sir," pleaded the boy. "He's been behaving a lot better lately than he used to do."

"There certainly was some room for improvement," returned the master, laughing. "Well, if you like to come to me again just before school, I'll go with you and speak to Mr. Westford."

The long summer afternoon dragged slowly away. Mullins brought Jack his dinner; and after that had been consumed, he sought to while away the hours of captivity by reading a tattered text-book on harmony, and strumming tunes with one finger on the piano. He wondered whether he would be sent away that evening or the following morning.

At length, just before the second tea-bell rang, the school porter once more appeared, this time to inform the prisoner that the headmaster wished to see him in his study. Mr. Westford sat at his table writing a letter, and received his visitor in grim silence.

"I've sent for you, sir," he said at length, "to tell you that I have been given to understand that you were not altogether to blame for what happened yesterday. There is, however, no excuse for your having set me at defiance by breaking the strict rule I laid down that no boy was to attend the fair. As I have already said, I believe you are not solely responsible for the disgraceful behaviour of which I received a complaint this morning. I shall not, therefore, expel you at once, as I at first intended, but I am writing to your father to inform him that your conduct is so far from satisfactory that I must ask him to remove you at the end of the present term. Until then, remember you are not to go beyond the gates without my permission."

"Well, I've got off better than I expected," said Jack, as he walked up and down the quadrangle, talking matters over with his cousin. "It was jolly good of you, Val, to go and speak up for me to the old man. Ward told me all about it. If it hadn't been for that, I should have been expelled at once. You've always been a good friend to me ever since I came here."

"I'm sorry to think you're going at all," returned the other. "I can't help feeling awfully mad with Raymond."

"Yes," answered Jack, "it wasn't all my fault; but there, it's just my luck. The guv'nor'll be in a fine wax; but I don't care. Only one thing I'm sorry for, and that is that this'll be my last holidays at Brenlands."

# CHAPTER XIII.

## A ROBBERY AT BRENLANDS.

"So at last he ran away, frightening the little birds in the hedge as he flew over the palings. 'They are afraid of me, because I am so ugly,' he said. So he closed his eyes, and flew still further."— *The Ugly Duckling.*

Whatever changes and alterations might take place in the outside world, Brenlands seemed always to remain the same. Coming there again and again for their August holidays, the children grew to think of it as a place blessed with eternal summer, where the flowers and green leaves never faded from one year's end to another, and such a thing as a cold, foggy winter day, with the moisture dripping from the trees, and the slush of slowly melting snow upon the ground, was a thing which could never have been possible, even in the memory of the oldest inhabitant. Better still, the welcome which greeted them on their arrival was always as warm as on previous occasions, and never fell one single degree during the whole of the visit.

In spite of all this, on that glad day when Queen Mab's court gathered once more round her cosy tea-table, Jack was not in his usual spirits, but appeared silent and depressed. The result of Mr. Westford's letter to his father had been a reply to the effect that, as he seemed determined to waste his opportunities at school, it would be decidedly the best thing for him to come home and find some more profitable employment for his time.

When tea was over he strolled out into the garden, and wandered moodily up and down the trim, box-bordered paths. To realize that one has done with school life for ever, that the book, as it were, is closed, and the familiar pages only to be turned again in memory, is enough to make any boy thoughtful; but it was not this exactly that weighed upon Jack's mind. He had grown to love Queen Mab and his cousins; the thought of being different from them became distasteful; and he had entertained some vague notion of turning over a new leaf, and becoming a respectable member of society. Now all his half-formed resolutions had come to the ground like a house of cards, and he was ending up worse than he had begun.

He was standing staring gloomily at the particular pear-tree which marked the scene of his and Valentine's first encounter with Joe Crouch, when his aunt came out and joined him.

"Well, Jack, and so you've left school for good?"

She made no mention of the Melchester fair incident, though Jack himself had sent her all particulars. He wished she would lecture him, for somehow her forbearance in not referring to the subject was worse than a dozen reproofs.

"Yes, aunt, they've thrown me out at last!"

"It will be dreadful when both of you have left Melchester. Valentine tells me that next Easter he expects to be going on to an army coach, to prepare for Sandhurst."

"Yes, I know," answered Jack, petulantly. "I'm always telling him what a lucky dog he is. I wish I had half his chances, and was going into the army, instead of back to that miserable Padbury."

"What does your father mean you to do?"

"Oh, he's got some scheme of sending me into the office of some metal works there. He says it's about all I'm good for, and he hasn't any money to put me in the way of learning a profession. But," added the boy impatiently, "he knows I hate the idea of grubbing away at a desk all day. I want to be a soldier."

"I know you do, and I believe you'd make a good one; but, after all, it would be a sad thing if every one devoted themselves to learning to fight. Besides, we can't afford to let all our gallants go to the wars; we want some to stay behind and do brave things in their daily life at home."

"Well, I'm not going to rust all my life in an office," answered Jack doggedly. "Rather than do that, I'll go off somewhere and enlist."

Queen Mab looked down and smiled. They were walking together arm in arm, and he was fumbling with the little bunch of trinkets on her watch chain.

"Do you recollect who gave me that little silver locket?"

"Yes," he answered, with a pouting smile.

"Well, then, please to remember that you are always going to be my own boy, and so don't talk any more about such things as running away and enlisting."

"Yes, but what am I to do? Look at the difference between my chances and Val's."

"I think that a man's success often depends more on himself, and less on circumstances, than you imagine," she answered. "'To be born in a duck's nest, in a farmyard, is of no consequence to a bird if it is hatched from a swan's egg.' That's what the story says that I used to tell the children."

Jack laughed, and shook his head. He was far from being convinced of the truth of this statement.

A few mornings later the usual harmony of the breakfast-table was disturbed by the arrival of a letter from Raymond Fosberton.

"He writes," said Miss Fenleigh, "to say that his father and mother are going away on a visit, and so he wants to come here for a few days."

The announcement was received with a chorus of groans.

"I wonder he has the cheek to come, after the way he treated us at Melchester," said Valentine; "I never wish to see him again."

Raymond did come, however, and instead of being at all abashed at the recollection of the termination of his tea-party, he was, if anything, more uppish than ever. It was only natural that he should make some reference to their adventure at the fair, and this he did by blaming Jack for not having made good his escape.

"Why didn't you run for it sooner, you duffer? You stood still there like a stuffed monkey, and wouldn't move till the man collared you."

"And you ran so far and so fast," retorted Jack, "that you couldn't get back to own up it was your doing, and save me from being expelled."

"Oh, go on! it isn't so bad as that," answered Raymond airily. "You ought to be jolly glad you're going to get out of that place. It's no good quarrelling over spilt milk.—Look here, will either of you do a chap a friendly turn? Can you lend me some money? I want a pound or two rather badly. Of course, I'd have got it from home, only the guv'nor's away."

Jack and Valentine shook their heads.

"Well, I wish you could," continued the other. "I'd give you a shilling in the pound interest, and pay you back for certain at the end of next month."

"I wonder how it is," said Jack to Valentine that evening as they were undressing, "that Raymond's always wanting money, and never seems to have any. His people are rich enough, and I should think they make him a good allowance."

"Of course they do," answered Valentine, "but he throws it away somehow; and he's the most selfish fellow in the world, and never spends a halfpenny on any one but himself."

Raymond was certainly no great addition to the party at Brenlands. His manners, one could well imagine, resembled those of the ferocious animal in the Fosberton crest, which capered on a sugar-stick with its tongue stuck out of its mouth, as though it were making faces at the world in general. He monopolized the conversation at table, voted croquet a bore, and spent most of his time lying under a tree smoking and reading a novel. He fell foul of Joe Crouch (who still came to do odd jobs in the garden) over some trifling matter, calling him an impudent blockhead, and telling Miss Fenleigh in a lofty manner that "he would never allow such a cheeky beggar to be hanging about the premises at Grenford."

"I am sick of the fellow," said Valentine to Helen that same evening. "I wish he wouldn't come here during the holidays; it spoils the whole thing."

On the following day Raymond was destined to give his cousins still more reason for wishing that he had not favoured Brenlands with a visit. At dinner he was full of a project for borrowing a gun, and having some target practice in the garden.

"I know a man living not far away who's got a nice, little, single-barrelled muzzle-loader. We might borrow it, and make some bullets, then stick up a piece of board against that hedge at the end of the long path, and have a regular shooting match."

"Oh, I don't want any guns here!" said Queen Mab. "I should be afraid that one of you might get hurt. You'd far better stick to your croquet."

"Yes," added Valentine. "It would be precious risky work firing bullets about in this garden with a muzzle-loader."

"Pooh! you're a nice chap to think of being a soldier, if you're afraid of letting off a gun!"

"Val knows a lot more about guns than you do," broke in Jack. "I suppose you think a thorn hedge and a bit of board would stop a bullet, you duffer!"

Raymond lost his temper, and the discussion was carried on in a manner which was more spirited than polite.

"Come, come," interposed Queen Mab, "I think we might change the subject. I'm sure Raymond won't want to borrow the gun if he knows it would make me nervous."

The meal was finished in silence. Anything so near a quarrel had never been known before at Brenlands, and proved very disturbing in what was usually such a peaceful atmosphere.

Jack sauntered out into the garden in no very tranquil frame of mind. Joe Crouch was there, weeding. They had always been good friends ever since the pear incident, and something in Jack's mode of action on that occasion seemed to have gained for him an abiding corner in Crouch's respect and affections.

"Well, Joe, what's the news?"

"Nothing particular that I knows of, sir, but there—there was somethin' I had to tell you; somethin' about this 'ere young bloke who comes orderin' every one around, as if the place was his own."

"What's that?"

"Why, I'll tell you," continued Crouch, lowering his voice in a significant manner. "You remember, sir, you was askin' me this time last year about a man called Hanks, who'd come up to you wantin' money, and you didn't know 'ow he'd got to know you. Well, he's in jail now for stealing fowls; but I seen him a month or so back, and got to know all about the whole business."

The speaker paused to increase the interest of his story.

"Well, what was it?"

"D'you remember, sir, about two years agone you and Master Valentine and the young ladies went up the river to a place called Starncliff? Well, Hanks said he saw you there, and that you set some one's rick afire. He wasn't sure which of you done it, but he had a word with Master Fosberton as you was comin' 'ome, and he told him it was you two had been smokin', but that you were his cousins, and he didn't want to get you into a row; so he said he'd give Hanks five shillings to hold his tongue, and promised he'd speak to you, and between you you'd make it up to something more, and that's why Hanks was always botherin' of you for money."

Jack's wrath, which had been quickly rising to boiling point during the recital of this narrative, now fairly bubbled over.

"What a lie!" he exclaimed. "What a mean cad the fellow is! Why, he set the rick on fire himself!"

"I just thought as much," said Joe.

"Yes, and that's not all. He knew we got into a row at school through the man talking to us; and then last summer, when the man was drunk, and met us in the road, he pretended he couldn't tell how it was the fellow knew our names!"

"Well, 'ere he is," interrupted Joe Crouch; "and if I was you, I'd just give him a bit of my mind!"

Raymond came sauntering across the lawn.

"I say," he exclaimed, "what a place this is! Fancy not being allowed to let off a gun. It's just what you might have expected from an old maid like Aunt Mabel, but I should have thought Valentine would have had more pluck. A fine sort of soldier he'll make—the milksop!"

Raymond Fosberton had for some time been running up an account in his cousin's bad books. This speech was the final entry, and caused Jack to demand an immediate settlement.

"Look here," he began, trembling with indignation, "don't you speak like that to me about Aunt Mab or Valentine, He's got a jolly sight more pluck than you have, you coward! If you want to begin calling names, I'll tell you yours—you're a liar and a sneak!"

"What d'you mean?"

"I mean what I say. I know all your little game, and it's no good your trying to keep it dark any longer. You told Hanks that Val and I had set that rick on fire, and so got us into a row through the man's speaking to us at Melchester. And last year, when we met him, you made out you didn't know why he should be always pestering us for money."

Raymond's face turned pale, but he made no attempt to deny the accusation.

"That was one of your cowardly tricks. Another was when you ran away after knocking that lamp over at the fair, the other day, and left Rosher and me to get out of the bother as best we could. That was what practically got me thrown out of the school. For two pins I'd punch your head, you miserable tailor's dummy!"

It was hardly likely that a fashionable young man like Master Raymond Fosberton would stand such language from a school-boy two years his junior.

"I should like to see you!" he remarked. "Two can play at that game."

The speaker did not know the person he was addressing; in another moment his request was granted. Jack came at him like a tiger, put all the force of his outraged feelings into a heavy right and left, and Raymond Fosberton disappeared with a great crash into a laurel bush.

Joe Crouch rose from his knees with a joyful exclamation, wiping his hands on his apron. "I should have liked to have had a cut in myself," he afterwards remarked, "but Master Jack he managed it all splendid!"

Whatever Joseph's wishes may have been, he had no opportunity of taking part in the proceedings; for, before the contest could be renewed, Helen rushed across the lawn and caught Jack by the arm.

"Oh, don't fight!" she cried breathlessly. "What is the matter?"

"Ask him!" answered Jack shortly, nodding with his fists still clenched, in the direction of Fosberton, who was in the act of emerging from the depths of the laurel bush. "Ask him, he knows."

"He called me a liar!" answered Fosberton; "and then rushed up and hit me when I was unprepared, the cad!"

This assertion very nearly brought on a renewal of the contest, but the speaker knew that Helen's presence would prevent any more blows being struck. Jack watched his adversary with a look of contempt, as the latter wiped the blood from his cut lip.

"Yes, I said you were a liar and a coward."

"Oh, hush!" said the girl, laying her hand on her cousin's mouth. "Don't quarrel any longer; it's dreadful here, at Brenlands! What would Aunt Mabel say if she knew you'd been fighting? Come away, Jack, and don't say any more."

The boy would have liked to stay behind for another private interview with Raymond, but for Helen's sake he turned on his heel and followed her into the house.

"All right, my boy," muttered Raymond, looking after the retreating figures with a savage scowl on his face, "I'll be even with you some day, if ever I get the chance."

There was a great lack of the usual mirth and gaiety at the tea-table that evening. Every one knew what had happened, and in their anxiety to avoid any reference to the painful subject conversation flagged, and even Queen Mab's attempts to enliven the assembly for once proved a failure. Neither of the boys would have been at all shocked at seeing a row settled by an exchange of blows, had the dispute taken place at school; but here, at Brenlands, it seemed a different matter—bad blood and rough language were out of keeping with the place, and the punching of heads seemed a positive crime.

To make matters worse, the day ended with a thunderstorm, and the evening had to be spent indoors. Raymond was in a sulk, and refused to join in any of the parlour games which were usually resorted to in wet weather.

"Aunt Mab, I wish you'd show us some of your treasures," said Barbara. She was kneeling upon a chair in front of a funny little semicircular cupboard with a glass door, let into the panelling of the wall, and filled with china, little Indian figures, and all kinds of other odds and ends.

"Very well, dear, I will," answered Miss Fenleigh, glad to think of some way of amusing her guests. "Run up and fetch the bunch of keys out of the middle drawer in my dressing-table."

The young people gathered round, and the contents of the cupboard were handed from one to another for examination. The curiosities were many and various. The girls were chiefly taken with the china; while what most appealed to Jack and Valentine was a small Moorish dagger. They carefully examined the blade for any traces of bloodstains, and trying the point against their necks, speculated as to what it must feel like to be "stuck."

"And what's that?" asked Barbara, pointing to a little, square leather case on the bottom shelf.

"Ah! that's the thing I value more than anything else," answered Queen Mab. "There!" she continued, opening the box and displaying a large, handsome gold watch. "That was given to your grandfather by the passengers on his ship at the end of one of his voyages to Australia. They met with dreadful weather, and I know I've heard him say that for two days and nights, when the storm was at its height, he never left the deck. You boys ought to be proud to remember it. There, Valentine, read the inscription."

The boy read the words engraved on the inside of the case:—

### Presented to
### CAPTAIN JOHN FENLEIGH,
### OF THE "EVELINA" STEAMSHIP,

As a small acknowledgment of the skill and ability displayed by him under circumstances of exceptional difficulty and danger.

"My father has a gold watch that was given to him when he retired from business," said Raymond; "it's bigger than that, and has got our crest on the back. By-the-bye," he continued, "aren't you afraid of having it stolen? I shouldn't keep it in that cupboard, it I were you. You are certain to get it stolen some day."

"Oh, we don't have any thieves at Brenlands," answered his aunt, smiling.

"I've a jolly good mind to steal it myself," said Jack; "or it you like, aunt, I'll exchange."

Jack's watch was always a standing joke against him, and, as he drew it out, the bystanders laughed. It was something like the timepiece by which, when the hands were at 9.30 and the bell struck three, one might know it was twelve o'clock. The silver case was dented and scratched; the long hand was twisted; the works, from having been taken to pieces and hurriedly put together again in class, were decidedly out of order; in fact, Jack was not quite certain if, when cleaning it on one occasion, he had not lost one of the wheels.

Queen Mab laughed and shook her head. "No, thank you," she said. "I think I should prefer to keep mine for the present, though one of you shall have it some day."

Raymond always came down to breakfast long after the others had finished. The next morning there was a letter waiting for him which had been readdressed on from Melchester. He was still in a sulk, and the contents of the epistle did not seem to improve his temper. He devoured his food in silence, and then went off by himself to smoke at the bottom of the garden.

"He is a surly animal," said Valentine. "I wish he had never come."

"Well, he's going to-morrow evening," answered Helen, "and I suppose we must make the best of him till then."

During the remainder of the day Raymond kept to himself, and though, after tea, he condescended to take part in some of the usual indoor games, he did it in so ungracious a manner as to spoil the pleasure of the other players.

Somehow the last day or so did not seem at all like the usual happy times at Brenlands. There was a screw loose somewhere, and every one was not quite so merry and good-tempered as usual.

"Bother it! wet again!" said Barbara, pushing back her chair from the breakfast-table with a frown and a pout.

"Never mind," answered her aunt. "Rain before seven, fine before eleven."

Barbara did not believe in proverbs. She wandered restlessly round the room, inquiring what was the good of rain in August, and expressing her discontent with things in general.

"Oh, I say," she exclaimed suddenly, halting in front of the little glass door of the cupboard, "what do you think has happened? That dear little china man with the guitar has tumbled over and broken his head off!"

Helen and the boys crowded round to look. It was certainly the case—the little china figure lay over on its side, broken in the manner already described.

"Who can have done it?"

"I expect I must have upset it the other evening when I was showing you the things," answered Miss Fenleigh. "Never mind, I think I can mend it. Go and fetch my keys, Bar, and we'll see just what's the matter with the little gentleman."

"This is funny," she continued, a few minutes later, "the key won't turn. Dear me! what a silly I am! why, the door isn't locked after all."

The little image was taken out, and while it was being examined Barbara picked up the little leather case on which it usually stood. In another moment she gave vent to an ejaculation of surprise which startled the remainder of the company, and made them immediately forget all about the china troubadour.

"Why, aunt, where's the watch?"

Every one looked. It was true enough—the case was empty, and the watch gone. For a moment there was a dead silence, the company being too much astonished to speak.

135

"Stolen!" exclaimed Raymond. "I said it would be some day."

"But when was it taken?—Who could have done it?—Where did they get in?—How did they know about it?"

These and other questions followed each other in rapid succession. A robbery at Brenlands! The thing seemed impossible; and yet here was the empty case to prove it. The watch had disappeared, and no one had the slightest notion what could have become of it.

"There's something in this lock," said Valentine, who had been peering into the keyhole. "Lend me your crochet needle, Helen, and I'll get it out."

With some little difficulty the obstacle was removed, and on examination proved to be a fragment of a broken key.

"Hallo!" said Raymond, "here's a clue at any rate. Don't lose it; put it in that little jar on the mantelpiece."

The remainder of the morning was passed in an excited discussion regarding the mysterious disappearance of the gold timepiece.

"I can't think any one can have stolen it," said Queen Mab. "How should they have known about it? and, besides, if any one broke into the house last night, how is it they didn't take anything else—that little silver box, for instance?"

"It's stolen, right enough," said Raymond. "It couldn't have been Joe Crouch, could it?"

"Not a bit of it," answered Jack decisively. "He wouldn't do a thing like that. He stole some fruit once, but he's honest enough now."

"Could the servant have taken it?"

"Oh, no!" answered Queen Mab. "I could trust Jane with anything."

During the afternoon the weather cleared, but no one seemed inclined to do anything; a feeling of gloom and uneasiness lay upon the whole company.

Jack was sitting in a quiet corner reading, when his aunt called him.

"Oh, there you are! I wanted to speak to you alone just for a minute. Helen told me about your quarrel with Raymond, and I want you to make it up. He's going away to-night, and I shouldn't like you to part, except as friends."

The boy frowned. "I don't want to be friends," he answered impatiently. "He's played me some very shabby tricks, and I think the less we see of him the better."

"Perhaps so; but I'm so sorry that you should have actually come to blows, and that while you were staying here with me at Brenlands."

"I'm not sorry! I wish I'd hit him harder!"

"Oh, you 'ugly duckling!'" answered the lady, smiling, and running her fingers through his crumpled hair. "You'll find out some day that 'punching heads,' as you call it, isn't the most satisfactory kind of revenge. However, I don't expect you to believe it now, but I think you'll do what I ask you. Go to Raymond, and say you're sorry you forgot yourself so far as to strike him, and ask his pardon. There, I don't think there is anything in that which need go against your conscience, or that it is a request that any gentleman need be ashamed to make."

Jack complied, but with a very bad grace. If the suggestion had come from any one but Queen Mab, he would have scouted the idea from the first.

He found Raymond swinging in a hammock under the trees.

"I say," he began awkwardly, "I'm sorry I hit you when we had that row. Aunt Mabel wished me to tell you so."

"Hum! You'll be sorrier still before long. I suppose now you want to 'kiss and be friends'?"

"No, I don't."

"Then if you don't want to be forgiven," returned the other with a sneer, "why d'you come and say you're sorry?"

137

Jack turned away in a rage, feeling that he had at all events got the worst of this encounter, and that it was entirely his own fault for having laid himself open to the rebuff.

He felt vexed with Helen for telling his aunt what had taken place, and with the latter for influencing him to offer Raymond an apology. Altogether the atmosphere around him seemed charged with discomfort and annoyance, and even the merry tinkle of the tea-bell was not so welcome as usual.

"Where's Raymond?" asked Queen Mab.

"I think he's putting his things in his bag," answered Valentine. "Shall I go and call him?"

At that moment the subject of their conversation entered the room. He walked round to his place in silence, pausing for a moment to take something down from the mantelpiece.

"Who owns a key with a scrap of steel chain tied on to it?"

"I do," answered Jack. "It belongs to my play-box."

"Well, here it is," returned the other. "I picked it up among the bushes. Do you notice anything peculiar about it?"

"No."

"You don't? Well, here's something belonging to it," and so saying, the speaker flipped across the table the little metal fragment which had been taken from the lock in the cupboard door.

"Confound it!" said Jack. "The thief must have used my key!"

"*Faugh!*" ejaculated Raymond, bitterly.

Jack looked up quickly with an expression of anger and astonishment.

"What's the matter?" he cried. "D'you mean to say I took the watch?"

"I've said nothing of the kind," answered the other coldly; "though I remember you did say you'd a good mind to steal it. I've simply given you back your key."

If a thunderbolt had fallen in the middle of the pretty tea-table, it could not have caused more astonishment and dismay than this last speech of Raymond's. Every one for the moment was too much taken aback to speak.

The smouldering fire of Jack's wrath had only needed this breeze to set it into a flame. His undisciplined spirit immediately showed itself in an outburst of ungovernable anger.

"You are a cad and a liar!" he said. "Wait till I get you outside."

"Hush! hush!" interrupted Miss Fenleigh, fearing a repetition of the previous encounter. "I can't have such words used here. Perhaps Raymond may be mistaken."

The last words were spoken thoughtlessly, in the heat of the moment. Jack in his anger resented that "may" and "perhaps," as implying doubt as to his honesty, and regarded the silence of the others as a sign that they also considered him guilty. In his wild, reckless manner he dashed his knife down upon the table, and with a parting glare at his accuser, marched straight out of the room.

Valentine rose to follow him.

"No, Val," said Miss Fenleigh, in an agitated voice. "Leave him to himself for a little while. He'll be calmer directly."

Ten minutes later the front door closed with a bang.

"He's going out to get cool, I suppose," said Raymond scornfully. "He didn't seem to relish my finding his play-box key. However, perhaps he'll explain matters when he comes back."

But Jack did not come back. The blind fury of the moment gave place to a dogged, unreasoning sense of wrong and injustice. He had been accused of robbing the person he loved best on earth, and she believed him to be guilty. The old, wayward spirit once more took full possession of his heart, and in a moment he was ready to throw overboard all that he prized most dearly.

He had some money in his pocket, enough to carry him home if he walked to Melchester, and his luggage could come on another time. The plan was formed, and he did not hesitate to put it into immediate execution.

It was not until nearly an hour after his departure that Queen Mab realized what had become of him, and then her distress was great.

"Why didn't he wait to speak to us!" she cried. "We must all write him a letter by to-night's post, to tell him that, of course, we don't think he's the thief, and to beg him to come back."

"If you like to do it at once," said Raymond, "I'll post them at Grenford. They'll reach him then the first thing in the morning."

The letters were written; even Barbara, who never could be got to handle a pen except under strong compulsion, scribbled nearly four pages, and filled up the blank space at the end with innumerable kisses.

About two hours later the scapegoat tramped, footsore and weary, into the Melchester railway station; and at nearly the same moment, Raymond Fosberton, on his way home, took from his pocket the letters which had been entrusted to his care, tore them to fragments, and dropped them over the low wall of a bridge into the canal.

"Now we're about quits!" he said.

# CHAPTER XIV.

## THE SOUND OF THE DRUM.

"'I believe I must go out into the world again,' said the duckling."— *The Ugly Duckling.*

The summers came and went, but Jack Fenleigh remained a rebel, refusing to join the annual gathering at Brenlands, and to pay his homage at the court of Queen Mab.

One bright September morning, about four years after the holidays described in the previous chapter, he was sitting at an untidy breakfast-table, evidently eating against time, and endeavouring to divide his attention between swallowing down the meal and reading a letter which lay open in front of him. The teapot, bread, butter, and other provisions had been gathered round him in a disorderly group, so as to be near his hand; the loaf was lying on the tablecloth, the bacon was cold, and the milk-jug was minus a handle. It was, on the whole, a very different display from the breakfast-table at Brenlands; and perhaps it was this very thought that crossed the young man's mind as he turned and dug viciously at the salt, which had caked nearly into a solid block.

In outward appearance, to a casual observer, Jack had altered very little since the day when he knocked Master Raymond Fosberton into the laurel bush; yet there was a change. He had broadened, and grown to look older, and more of a man, though the old impatient look seemed to have deepened in his face like the lines between his eyebrows.

The party at Brenlands had waited in vain for a reply to their letters. Within a week, Miss Fenleigh had written again, assuring the runaway that neither she nor his cousins for one moment suspected him of having stolen the watch; but in the meantime the mischief had been done.

"They think I did it," muttered Jack to himself, "or they'd have written at once. Aunt Mabel wants to forgive me, and smooth it over; but they know I'm a scamp, and now they believe I'm a thief!"

Again he hardened his heart, and though his feelings towards Queen Mab and his cousins never changed, yet his mind was made up to cut himself adrift from the benefit of their society. He left Valentine's letter unanswered, and refused all his aunt's pressing invitations to visit her again.

Every year these were renewed with the same warmth and regularity, and it was one which now lay open beside his plate.

"I suppose," ran the letter, "that you have heard how well Val passed out of Sandhurst. He is coming down to see me before joining his regiment, and will bring Helen and Barbara with him. I want you to come too, and then we shall all be together once more, and have the same dear old times over again. I shan't put up with any excuses, as I know you take your holiday about this time, so just write and say when you are coming."

Jack lifted his eyes from the letter, and made a grab at the loaf.

"I should like to go," he muttered; "how jolly the place must look!—but no, I've left it too long. I ought to have gone back at once, or never to have run away like that. Of course, now they must think that I stole the watch. Yet, perhaps, if I gave them my word of honour, they'd believe me; I know Aunt Mabel would."

At this moment the door opened, and a gentleman entered the room. He was wearing a shabby-looking dressing-gown, a couple of ragged quill pens were stuck in his mouth, and he carried in his hand a bundle of closely-written sheets of foolscap. Mr. Basil Fenleigh, to tell the truth, was about to issue an invitation to a "few friends" to join him in starting an advertisement and bill-posting agency business; to be conducted, so said the rough copy of the circular, on entirely novel lines, which could not fail to ensure success, and the drafting out of which had occupied most of his leisure time during the past twelve months.

"Humph!" he exclaimed sourly. "Down at your usual time, eh? You'll be late again at your office."

"No, I shan't," answered the son, glancing up at the clock. "I can get there in ten minutes."

"You can't. You know very well Mr. Caston complained only the other day of your coming behind your time. The next thing will be that you'll lose your situation."

"I don't care if I do; I'm heartily sick of the place."

"You're heartily sick of any kind of work, and you always have been."

Jack threw down his knife and fork and rose from the table, leaving part of his breakfast unfinished on his plate.

"All right," he said sulkily; "I'll go at once."

He strode out of the room, crushing Queen Mab's letter into a crumpled ball of paper in his clenched fist. After what had just passed, he would certainly not broach the subject of a holiday.

The morning's work seemed, if possible, more distasteful than ever. Casting up sheets of analysis, he got wrong in his additions, and had to go over them again. He watched the workmen moving about in the yard outside, and wished he had been trained to some manual trade like theirs. Then he thought of Valentine, and for the first time his affection for his old friend gave place to a feeling of bitterness and envy.

"Confound the fellow! he's always done just as he liked. I wish he was here in my shoes for a bit. It isn't fair one chap should have such luck, and another none at all. Little he cares what becomes of me. I may rot here all my life, and no one troubles the toss of a button whether I'm happy or miserable."

He was in the same ill-humour when he returned home to dinner. Mr. Fenleigh was also out of temper, and seemed inclined to give vent to his feelings by renewing the dispute which had commenced at the breakfast-table. Father and son seldom met except at meals; and unfortunately, on these occasions, the conversation frequently took the form of bickering and complaint. Jack, as a rule, appeared sullenly indifferent to what passed; this time, however, his smouldering discontent burst out into a name of anger.

"I suppose you *were* late this morning?"

"No, I wasn't."

"Humph! You said before you started that you were sick of the place, and didn't care whether you lost it. If you do, I hope you won't expect me to find you another berth."

"No, I'll find one myself."

"What d'you think you're good for? You're more likely to idle about here doing nothing than find any other employment."

"I work harder than you do," said the son angrily.

"Hold your tongue, sir! If you can't treat me with some amount of respect, you'd better leave the house."

"So I will. I'll go and enlist."

"You may go where you please. I've done the best I could for you, and all the return I get is ingratitude and abuse. Now you can act for yourself."

It was not the first time that remarks of this character had been fired across the table. Jack made no reply, but at that moment his mind was seized with a desperate resolve. Once for all he would settle this question, and change the present weary existence for something more congenial to his taste. All that afternoon he turned the plan over in his thoughts, and his determination to follow it up grew stronger as the time approached for putting it into execution. What if the move were a false one? a person already in the frying-pan could but jump into the fire; and any style of life seemed preferable to the one he was now living. His father had told him to please himself, and, as he had only himself to consider, he would do so, and follow the drum, as had always been his inclination from childhood.

The big bell clanged out the signal for giving over work; but Jack, instead of returning home, picked up a small handbag he had brought with him, and walked off in the direction of the railway station. On his way thither, he counted the money in his pocket. He had some idea of going to London, but the expense of the journey would be too heavy for his resources. It mattered little where the plunge was taken; he would go to the barracks at Melchester.

He lingered for a moment at the window of the booking-office, hardly knowing why he hesitated.

Why not? He had only himself to please.

The clerk grew impatient. "Well?" he said.

Jack threw down his money. "Third, Melchester!" he said, and so crossed the Rubicon.

Very few changes had taken place in the little city during the four years which had elapsed since he last visited it. Here and there a house had been modernized, or a new shop-front erected, but in the neighbourhood of the school no alterations seemed to have been made. He strolled past it in the dusk, and paused to look in through the gates: the boys had not yet returned, and the quadrangle was dark and deserted. He thought of the night when he and Rosher had climbed in by way of the headmaster's garden, and forced an entry into the house through the bathroom window. It seemed a hardship then to be obliged to be in by a certain time, yet it was preferable to having no resting-place to claim as one's own.

A few minutes later he halted again, this time outside the well-remembered cookshop. "Duster's" was exactly the same as it always had been, except for the fact that, it being holiday time, the display of delicacies in the window was not quite so large as usual. Jack smiled as there flashed across his mind the memory of the literary society's supper; the faces of the sprightly Tinkleby, Preston the bowler, "Guzzling Jimmy," and a host of others, rose before him in the deepening twilight. They had been good comrades together once; most of them had probably made a fair start by this time in various walks of life. He wondered if they remembered him, and what they would say if they knew what he was doing, and whether any of them would care what became of him. No, he had only himself to please now, and if he preferred soldiering to office-work, what was there to hinder him from taking the shilling?

There was no particular hurry. He passed the night at a small temperance hotel, and next morning, after a plain breakfast, started out for a stroll into the country. He had written a note to his father before leaving Padbury merely stating his intention, and giving no address. There was nothing more to be done but to enjoy himself as a free man before making application to the nearest recruiting sergeant.

He passed the barracks where the 1st Battalion of the Royal Blankshire Regiment was quartered, and thought how often he and Valentine had lingered there, listening to the bugle-calls, and watching the drill instructors at work in the square with their awkward squads. Just inside the gate the guard were falling in, preparatory to the arrival of the relief, and something in their smart appearance, and in the very clank of their rifle-butts upon the flagstones, stirred his heart; yes, that was the calling he meant to follow.

He strode off along the Hornalby road, whistling a lively tune, and conjuring up bright mental pictures of the life before him. He might not have Valentine's luck, but he would make up for it in other ways. The path was steep and rough, no doubt, but in treading it scores of brave men had won honour and renown; and with courage and determination, there was no reason why he should not do the same. It was a man's life, and here there was certainly more chance of distinguishing oneself than in a manufacturer's office.

With these and other thoughts of a similar nature occupying his mind, Jack tramped on gaily enough in the bright sunshine. Suddenly, however, he stopped dead in the middle of the road. He had come in sight of a wayside inn, the Black Horse, and the thought struck him that he was within two miles of Brenlands.

All unbidden, a host of recollections came rushing upon him. The last time he had walked from Melchester along this road was the afternoon on which he brought back the silver locket for Queen Mab. What if the pony-carriage should suddenly turn the corner? and yet, why should he be afraid to meet her? He was doing nothing to be ashamed of, and the recollection of the stolen watch never entered his head. He would have given anything to have gone on and seen her again—to have had one more kind smile and loving word. "My own boy Jack!" Would he ever hear her say that again?

He turned on his heel, and began the return journey with a gloomy look of discontent upon his face. His castles in the air had vanished: what was there that made a soldier's life attractive but the right to go about in a red coat like a barrel-organ monkey? For two pins he would abandon the project, and go back to Padbury.

This impression, however, was not destined to last very long. As he approached the barracks he noticed a small crowd of idlers collecting near a gateway, and at the same instant the silence was broken by the sound of a drum. He knew what it was—the regiment had been out drilling on the neighbouring common, and was on its way home.

He hurried forward to watch the soldiers as they passed.

Boom! boom! boom!—boom! boom! boom! With a glorious crash the brass instruments burst out with the tune. Jack knew it well, and his heart danced to it as the band marched out into the road.

"'Twas in the merry month of May,
When bees from flower to flower did hum,
Soldiers through the town marched gay,
The village flew to the sound of the drum!"

Jack drew back into the hedge to watch as the regiment went by.

"March at ease!" The sunlight flashed as the arms were sloped, and glittered on bright blades as the officers returned their swords. Not a detail escaped his eager observation; the swing of the rifle-barrels, the crisp tramp of the marching feet, even the chink of the chain bridles as the horses of the mounted officers shook their heads, all seemed to touch answering chords in his inmost heart, and awaken there the old love and longing for a soldier's life.

"The tailor he got off his knees,
And to the ranks did boldly come:
He said he ne'er would sit at ease,
But go with the rest, and follow the drum!"

Jack hesitated no longer, but hurried back to pick up the few belongings he had left at the hotel, determined to put his project into execution without further delay.

# CHAPTER XV.

## THE QUEEN'S SHILLING.

"If he had called out, 'Here I am,' it would have been all right; but he was too proud to cry out for help while he wore a uniform."—*The Brave Tin Soldier.*

There was no more hesitation or uncertainty about his movements now, and before he knew it, Jack found himself once more back at the barracks. The corporal on "gate duty," who, for want of something better to do, had been chastising his own leg with a "swagger cane," ceased in the performance of this self-imposed penance, and shot a significant glance at the stranger.

"Looking out for any one?" he inquired, by way of opening up a conversation.

"No," answered Jack; "the fact is, I've come to enlist. D'you think you could make a soldier of me?"

"Well, at any rate, I should say you were big enough," answered the corporal briskly. "Why, we ought to make a general of a smart young fellow like you, in less than no time!"

This seemed a promising commencement; but the adjutant, in front of whom Jack was conducted after undergoing a preliminary examination as to his height, chest measurement, and strength of eyesight, did not appear to be of quite so sanguine a temperament as the non-commissioned officer.

He eyed the would-be recruit with no very favourable expression on his face, as he prepared to take down the answers to the questions on the attestation paper.

"Name?"

"John Fenleigh."

"Is that a *nom de guerre*?"

"No, sir, it's my real name."

"Humph! So you speak French?"

Jack coloured slightly.

"No, sir—that is, I learned some at school."

The officer looked up, and laid his quill pen down on the table.

"Look here, my good fellow," he said, "it's not my business to ask what brings you here, but one thing I should like to know: how long do you expect you are going to remain in the army—a week, or six months?"

"The full time, I hope, sir."

"Are your parents living? And do they know of the step you're taking?"

"My father is living. I told him what I meant to do before I left home."

"Well," returned the officer, once more dipping his quill in the ink, "if you change your mind before to-morrow, you'll have to pay a sovereign; after that, it'll cost you ten pounds!"

The paper was filled up, and our hero received the historical shilling, which he slipped into his waistcoat pocket, having previously determined never to part with that particular coin, unless he were obliged. He was then conducted to the hospital, and there examined by the medical officer; his eyesight being once more tested by his having to count a number of white dots on a piece of black paper displayed on the opposite side of the room, each eye being covered alternately.

Having passed satisfactorily through this ordeal, he was informed that he could not be sworn in before the following day, when he must present himself at the orderly room at eleven o'clock. Until that time he was free to do as he pleased; and being still in the possession of the greater portion of his previous week's salary, he chose to sleep another night at the hotel, and so spent the remainder of the day wandering about the streets of Melchester.

On the following morning, at the appointed hour, he returned to the barracks, and after some little delay, was brought into the presence of the commanding officer, where he was duly "sworn in," and signed his name to the declaration of allegiance.

"You'll join C Company," said the sergeant-major. "Just take him across, orderly, and show him the room."

With feelings very much akin to those of the "new boy" arriving for the first time at a big boarding-school, our hero followed his guide across the square, up a flight of stairs, and down a long corridor, amid a good deal of noise and bustle. The bugle had not long since sounded "Come to the cook-house door," and the dinner orderlies were hurrying back with the supply of rations for their respective rooms.

At length a door was reached, in front of which the orderly paused with, "Here you are!" Jack entered, and made his first acquaintance with his future home—the barrack-room.

It was large and lofty, with whitewashed walls and a floor of bare boards. A row of wooden tables and forms ran down the centre, above which was a hanging shelf for the men's plates and basins. Around the room were sixteen small iron bedsteads, each made in such a fashion that one half closed up under the other, the mattress when not in use being rolled up and secured by a strap, with the blankets and sheets folded on the top; the remaining portion of the couch, on which the rug was laid, serving for a seat. Above the bed were shelves and hooks for accoutrements, and other possessions. Above some of the cots small pictures or photographs were hung, which served to relieve the monotony of the whitewash; but these, like the rest of Tommy Atkins's property, were arranged with that scrupulous care and neatness which is so characteristic of all that concerns the service from baton to button-stick.

At the moment Jack entered, his future room-mates were busy round one end of the tables, assisting the orderly man in the task of pouring soup from a large can into the small basins, and making a similar equal division of the meat and potatoes. The new-comer's arrival, therefore, was scarcely noticed, except by the sergeant, who told him to sit down, and saw that he received a share of the rations. The fare was certainly rough, and seemed in keeping with the table manners of the rank and file of the Royal Blankshire; they forbore to "trouble" each other for things out of reach, but secured them with a dive and a grab. "Here, chuck us the rooty!" was the request when one needed bread; while though substantial mustard and pepper pots adorned the board, the salt was in the primitive form of a lump, which was pushed about from man to man, and scraped down with the dinner knives.

But Jack had not come to barracks expecting a *table d'hôte* dinner of eight or nine courses, served by waiters in evening dress, and he set to work with a good grace on what was set before him. The remarks addressed to him, if a trifle blunt, were good-natured enough, and he replied to them in the same spirit. His comrades evidently remarked from the first that he was a cut above the ordinary recruit; but he was wise enough to avoid showing any airs, and soon saw that this line of conduct was appreciated.

The meal was in progress when there was a sharp rap, and the door was opened.

"'Tenshun!" The men laid down their knives and forks, and rose to their feet.

"Dinners all right here?"

"Yes, sir."

"All present?"

"All present, sir." The orderly officer glanced round the room, and then turned and walked out.

"'E's a gentleman, is Mr. Lawson," murmured one of the men; "'e always shuts the door behind 'im." Jack's eye followed the figure of the lieutenant as he rejoined the orderly sergeant in the passage. It was not so much the sash and sword, and neat, blue patrol jacket, as the cheery voice and pleasant sunburnt face, which had attracted our hero's attention; somehow these reminded him of Valentine, and turned his thoughts back to his old friend. He wondered how his cousin looked in the same uniform. Well, well, however wide and deep the gulf might be which the doings of the last two days had placed between them, they were, in a way, reunited; for the service was the same, whatever difference there might be in shoulder-straps.

Dinner over, some of the men made down their beds for a nap, while others announced their intention "to do some soldiering," a term which implied the cleaning and polishing of accoutrements.

Sergeant Sparks, the non-commissioned officer in charge of the room, had a few friendly words with Jack, told him what he would have to do on the following day, and advised him in the meantime to make himself as comfortable as he could. "Here," he added, turning to a private, "just show this man his cot, and explain to him how to keep his bedding; you may want a good turn yourself some time."

The soldier obeyed readily enough. Jack had already caught his eye several times during dinner, and now followed him into a corner of the room, resolved if possible to patch up a friendship. In the carrying out of this intention he was destined to experience a startling surprise.

The man paused before one of the end beds, and began to unfasten the strap of the mattress.

"I didn't think of meeting you here, Mr. Fenleigh."

Jack started and stared at the speaker in silent astonishment.

"You remember me, sir?—Joe Crouch."

"What! Joe Crouch, who used to work at Brenlands?"

"Yes, sir; Joe Crouch as stole the pears," answered the soldier, smiling. "I never expected to find you 'listin' in the army, sir. I suppose Miss Fenleigh ain't aware of what you're doin'?"

"Oh, no!" exclaimed the other eagerly. "Promise me you'll never tell any one at Brenlands where I am—swear you won't."

"Very well, sir," replied Joe Crouch, calmly proceeding to unroll the mattress and make down the bed.

"For goodness' sake, drop that *sir*. Look here, Joe: I'm a lame dog, down on my luck, and no good to anybody; but we were friendly years ago, and if you'll have me for a comrade now, I'll do my best to be a good one."

Joe flung down the bedding, and held out his big, brown hand.

"That I will!" he answered. "You did the square thing by me once, and now I'll see you through; don't you fret."

Tea in barracks was evidently a very informal meal, of which no great account was taken. As Jack sat down to his bowl and chunk of bread, Joe Crouch pushed a screw of paper in front of him, which on examination proved to contain a small pat of butter.

"What's this?" asked Jack.

"Fat," answered Joe, shortly. "From the canteen," he added.

"Then you've paid for it, and—look here—you've got none yourself."

"Don't want any," answered Joe, breaking up a crust and dropping it into his tea. "There you are. That's what's called a 'floatin' battery.'"

In the evening most of the men went out. Jack, however, preferred to remain where he was, and passed the time reading a paper he had brought with him, at one of the tables. Sergeant Sparks came up to him and chatted pleasantly for half an hour. He wore a ribbon at his breast, and had stirring stories to tell of the Afghan war, and Roberts' march to Candahar. About half-past eight the men began to return from their walks and various amusements, and the barrack-room grew more noisy. At half-past nine the roll was called, and the orders read out for the following day, and Jack was not sorry when the time came to turn in. Crouch came over to see if he understood the preparation of his cot.

"The feathers in these 'ere beds grew on rather a large bird," remarked Joe, referring to the straw mattress, "but they're soft enough when you come off a spell of guard duty or a day's manoeuvrin'."

The bugle sounded the long, melancholy G, and the orderly man turned off the gas. Our hero lay awake for some time listening to the heavy breathing of his new comrades, and then turned over and fell asleep.

The bright morning sunshine was streaming in through the big windows when the clear, ringing notes of reveille and the cheery strains of "Old Daddy Longlegs" roused him to consciousness of where he was.

"Now then, my lads, show a leg there!" cried the sergeant.

Jack stretched and yawned. Yes, it was certainly a rough path, but his mind was made up to tread it with a good heart, and this being the case, he was not likely to turn back.

# CHAPTER XVI.

## ON ACTIVE SERVICE.

"A voice cried out, 'I declare here is the tin soldier!'"—*The Brave Tin Soldier.*

A brilliant, clear sky overhead, and such a scorching sun that the air danced with the heat, as though from the blast of a furnace; surely this could not be the twenty-fifth of December!

But Christmas Day it was—Christmas Day in the camp at Korti.

Among the pleasant groves of trees which bordered the steep banks of the Nile glistened the white tents of the Camel Corps. Still farther back from the river lay fields of grass and patches of green dhurra; and behind these again an undulating waste of sand and gravel, dotted here and there with scrub and rock, and stretching away to the faintly-discerned hills of the desert. The shade of the trees tempered the heat, making a pleasant change after the roasting, toilsome journey up country.

Here, though hardly to be recognized with their ragged clothing and unshaven faces, was gathered a body of men who might be regarded as representing the flower of England's army—Life Guards, Lancers, Dragoons, Grenadiers, Highlanders, and linesmen from many a famous foot regiment; all were there, ready to march and fight shoulder to shoulder in order to rescue Gordon from his perilous position in Khartoum.

"It was Christmas Day in the camp at Korti."

Every day the numbers in camp had been gradually growing larger, fresh batches of troops arriving either on camels or in boats. A whole fleet of these "whalers" lay moored along the bank of the Nile; the usual quiet of the river being continually broken by the dog-like panting of steam launches hurrying up and down the stream.

Friendly natives, clad in loose shirts and skull-caps, wandered through the lines, gazing wonderingly at all they saw; while in strange contrast to their unintelligible jabberings, rose the familiar *patois* of the barrack-room, or snatches of some popular music-hall song hummed or whistled by every urchin in the streets of London.

The concentration of the expedition had now been almost completed, and the chief topic of conversation was the immediate prospect of a desert march to Shendy.

But to return to our commencement, Christmas Day it was; and however difficult it might have been to realize this as far as the weather was concerned, the fact had, to a certain extent, been impressed upon the minds of the men by the supplementing of their ordinary dinner rations with a gallant attempt at plum-pudding, manufactured for the most part out of boiled dates.

Two men, who had just partaken of this delicacy, were lying stretched out full length under a shady tree, their pith helmets brought well forward over their eyes, their grey serge jumpers thrown open, and pipes in their mouths. To see them now, with their tattered nether garments, stubbly chins, and sunburnt faces, from which the skin was peeling off in patches, one could hardly have recognized in them the same smart soldiers who paraded a few months ago on the barrack square at Melchester. Yet such they were, as the reader will soon discover by the opening remarks of their conversation.

"This weather don't seem very seasonable. I wonder whether it's frost and snow away home at Brenlands."

"Yes; I wonder if the reservoir at Hornalby is frozen. We used to go skating there when I was at school. It seems a jolly long time ago now!"

"It don't seem three years ago to me since you enlisted. I never thought you'd have stayed so long."

"Didn't you? When my mind's made up, it's apt to stick to it, Joe, my boy. Besides, I had no prospect of anything better."

There was a pause, during which the two comrades (who, from the foregoing, will have been recognized as our hero and Joe Crouch) continued to puff away at their pipes in silence, listening to the remarks of three men who were playing a drowsy game with a tattered pack of cards.

"These cards are gettin' precious ragged; you'd better get 'em clipped."—"Why don't you play the king?"—"'Cause there ain't one! he's one of 'em as is lost."

"You used to have fine times, I reckon, when you and Mr. Valentine and the young ladies came to stay at Miss Fenleigh's," said Crouch. "I wonder what she'd say if she knew you was out here in Egypt."

"I took precious good care she shouldn't know. I suppose she heard from the guv'nor that I went off and enlisted, but I didn't send word what regiment I joined. I never mean to see her again—no fear!"

"She was a kind lady," murmured Joe reflectively; "very good to me once upon a time."

"Yes, that she was—the best and kindest woman in the world; and that's just the reason why I'm glad to think she doesn't know what's become of me.— Hallo, Swabs, what are you after?"

The person thus addressed was a gaunt, lanky-looking warrior, clad simply in helmet, shirt, and trousers; the sleeves of his "greyback" were rolled up above his elbows; and he was armed with a roughly-made catapult, evidently intended for the destruction of some of the small, brightly-coloured birds that were flitting about among the branches of the palms. "Swabs," who answered at roll-call to the name of Smith H., in addition to holding the badge as best shot in the regiment, was a popular character in C Company.

"Shist!" he answered; "when there ain't nothink better to shoot at, I'm goin' to try me 'and on some of these dickies."

"Swabs" was evidently more skilful with the rifle than with his present weapon. He discharged his pebble, but with no result.

"Miss; high right," said Jack. "Where did you get your elastic from?"

"The tube of me filter. I'll take a finer sight next time," and "Swabs" went stalking off in search of further sport.

"It seems hard to imagine that we're on the real business at last," said Jack, clasping his hands behind his head and stretching out his legs. "After so many sham fights, it seems rum to think of one in real earnest. The strange thing to me," he continued, "is to think how often my cousin and I used to talk about war, and wonder what it was like; and we thought he was the one more likely to see it. I used to be always grumbling about his luck, and now I expect he'd envy me mine."

"I suppose he hasn't come out?"

"No, I don't think so. I forget just where he's stationed. Look at Tom Briggs over there, he using his towel to put a patch on the seat of his breeches. Hey, Tommy! how are you going to dry yourself when you wash?"

"Wash!" answered the man, looking up from his work with a grin, "you'll be glad enough afore long to lap up every spot of water you come across; there won't be much talk of washin' in this 'ere desert, I'm thinkin'."

The answer was lost on Jack; something else had suddenly attracted his attention. He sat up and made a movement as though he would rise to his feet. An officer had just strolled past, wearing a fatigue cap and the usual serge jumper. His face was tanned a deep brown, and showed up in strong contrast to his fair hair and small, light-coloured moustache. Our hero's first impulse was to run after and accost the stranger, but he checked himself, and sank back into his former position.

"I say, Briggs," he called, "what men were those who came up in the boats yesterday?"

"Some of the ——sex Regiment," answered the other, stooping forward to bite off his cotton with his teeth.

Jack's heart thumped heavily, and he caught his breath; his eyes had not deceived him, and the subaltern who had just walked by was Valentine.

He was roused from his reverie by the warning call to "stables," it being the time for feeding and grooming the camels. They were queer steeds, these "ships of the desert," and for those who had never ridden them before even mounting and dismounting was no easy task. In the case of the former, unless the animals' heads were brought round to their shoulders, and held there by means of the rope which served as a rein, they were apt to rise up suddenly before the rider had got properly into the saddle, a proceeding usually followed by disastrous results; while, on the other hand, the sudden plunge forward as they dropped on their knees, followed by the lurch in the opposite direction when their hind-quarters went down, made it an extremely easy matter to come a cropper in either direction. Their necks seemed to be made of indiarubber, and their hind legs, with which they could scratch the top of their heads, or, if so inclined, kick out behind, even when lying down, appeared to be furnished with double joints. Jack had christened his mount "Lamentations," from the continual complaints which it uttered; but in this the animal was no worse than the remainder of its fellows, who bellowed and roared whatever was happening, whether they were being unsaddled, groomed, mounted, or fed.

With thoughts centred on his recent discovery, our hero made his way to the spot where the camels of his detachment were picketed, and there went mechanically through the work of cleaning up the lines, and the still more unsavoury task of attending to "Lam's" toilet. Should he speak to Valentine, or not? That was the question which occupied his mind. Unless he did so, it was hardly likely that after seven years, and with a moustache and sprouting beard, his cousin would recognize him among the seventeen hundred men destined to form the expedition.

The men marched back to their lines, and were then dismissed for tea. Jack sat silently sipping at his pannikin and munching his allowance of biscuit.

Should he speak to Valentine, or not? The vague day-dream of their school-boy days was realized—they were soldiers together, and on active service; but everything was altered now. The great difference of rank was, of itself, sufficient to place an impassable barrier between them; and then the recollection of their last parting, his refusals to meet his cousins again at Brenlands, and the fact of his having left so many of his old chum's letters unanswered, all seemed to lead up to one conclusion. Valentine would long ago have come to regard it as a clear proof that the runaway had really stolen the watch, and not have been surprised to hear that he had gone to the dogs. Nor was he likely now to be very well pleased if the black sheep suddenly walked up and claimed relationship. No. Jack felt he had long ago severed all ties with what had once been dear to him; it was the better plan to let things remain as they were, and make no attempt to renew associations with a past which could not be recalled.

Sunset was rapidly followed by darkness. In honour of its being Christmas Day, an impromptu concert had been announced; and the men began to gather round a rough stage which had been erected under the trees, and which was lit up with lamps and the glare of two huge bonfires.

The programme was of the free-and-easy character: volunteers were called for, and responded with songs, step-dances, and the like; while the audience, lying and sitting round on the sand, greeted their efforts with hearty applause, and joined in every chorus with unwonted vigour.

Jack had always possessed a good voice, a fact which had long ago been discovered by his comrades, and now, for the honour of the Royal Blankshire, those standing near him insisted that he should sing. Before he knew it, he was pushed forward, and hoisted on to the platform. There was no chance of retreat. He glanced round the sea of faces glowing brightly in the firelight, and after a moment's thought as to what would be likely to go down best, he struck up his old song, "The Mermaid."

"Oh! 'twas in the broad Atlantic, 'mid the equinoctial gales,
That a gay young tar fell overboard, among the sharks and whales."

The great crowd of listeners burst out into the "Rule, Britannia!" chorus with a mighty roar. But our hero heeded them not; his thoughts had suddenly gone back to the little parlour at the back of "Duster's" shop; his eyes wandered anxiously over the faces of the officers who were grouped together in front of the stage, but Valentine did not appear to be among them.

An uproarious repetition of the last "Rule, Britannia!" was still in progress as Jack rejoined the Blankshire contingent, and submitted his back to a number of congratulatory slaps.

These signs of approval were still being showered down upon him, when Sergeant Sparks touched his elbow.

"Here's an officer wants to speak to you, Fenleigh. There he is, standing over by that tree."

With his heart in his mouth, the singer stepped out of the crush, and approached the figure standing by itself under the heavy shadow of the palm.

"Jack!"

The private soldier made no reply, but raised his hand in the customary salute. The action was simple enough, and yet full of meaning, showing the altered relationship between the two old friends.

"Why, man, didn't you tell us where you were? and what had become of you?"

"There was no need; and, besides, I didn't wish you to know, sir?"

"Surely you are not still offended over what happened that summer at Brenlands? You must have known that we, none of us, suspected you for a moment of having stolen that watch. It was only a cad like Raymond Fosberton would ever have thought of suggesting such a thing."

"Appearances were very much against me, sir—and—well, it's all past and done with now."

Valentine was silent. That "sir," so familiar to his ear, and yet seemingly so incongruous in the present instance, baffled him completely. In the first moment of his discovery he had intended, figuratively speaking, to fall upon the prodigal's neck, and converse with him in the old, familiar style; but now, between Valentine Fenleigh, Esq., of the —— sex, and Private Fenleigh, of the Royal Blankshire, there was a great gulf fixed, and the latter, especially, seemed determined to recognize that the former conditions of their friendship could now no longer exist. After a moment's pause, Jack spoke.

"Could you tell me, sir, if they are all well?"

"Who? my people? They're all right, thanks. Helen's just gone and got married; and little Bar's just the same as ever, only a bit older. She was twenty-one last month."

Jack smiled. "And Aunt Mabel, have you seen her lately?"

"Oh, yes! she's very well, and doesn't seem to alter at all. She often talks of you, and is always sad because you never write. Why have you never been to see her?"

"I have seen her once. I passed her in the street in Melchester; but I was in uniform, and she didn't notice me."

"But why didn't you go over to Brenlands?"

"Oh, I couldn't do that! I struck out a path for myself. It may be a bit rough, like the way of transgressors always is; but it suits me well enough. I've been in it now for three years, and mean to stick to it; but it'll never bring me to Brenlands again."

"Oh, yes, it will," answered the other cheerily, "At the end of the long lane comes the turning."

There was another pause; the conversation had been running more freely, but now Jack fell back again into his former manner.

"I beg pardon, sir, but I should like to ask if you'll be good enough not to mention my name in any of your letters home."

"Why not?"

"I should be glad, sir, if you wouldn't. I've managed hitherto to keep my secret."

"Well, if it's your wish, for the present I won't," answered Valentine; "but if we both live through this business, then I shall have something to say to you on the subject."

"Good-night, sir."

"Good-night, old chap, and good luck to us both!"

# CHAPTER XVII

## UNDER FIRE.

"The tin soldier trembled; yet he remained firm; his countenance did not change; he looked straight before him, and shouldered his musket."—*The Brave Tin Soldier.*

Five days afterwards the camp was all astir, and presented an unusual scene of activity and animation.

On the twenty-eighth of December, orders had been issued for a portion of the force to march across the desert and occupy the wells at Gakdul; and on this, the morning of the thirtieth, the Guards Camel Regiment and the Mounted Infantry (to which latter force Jack and his comrades of the Royal Blankshire were attached), together with detachments of the Engineers and Medical Staff Corps, a squadron of the 19th Hussars, and a large train of "baggagers," were preparing for the start, amid much bugle-blowing, shouting of orders, and roaring of camels as the loads were being placed on their backs. Gradually, as the hour approached for the assembly of the force, the noise grew less; even "Lamentations" ceased his protestations, and stalked off to the parade ground without further murmuring.

Lord Wolseley inspected the force, and shortly before three o'clock the cavalry scouts started. As Jack stood by the side of his kneeling steed, with Joe Crouch on his right, his heart beat fast. This was something different from any of his previous military experiences; the cartridges in his pouch and bandoleer were ball, not blank. It was to be the real thing this time; the stern reality of what he and Valentine had so often pictured and played at far away in the peaceful old house at Brenlands.

Though showing it in different ways, all his comrades were more or less excited at the prospect of a move: some were silent, others unusually noisy; Joe Crouch puffed incessantly at a little clay pipe; Sergeant Sparks seemed to have grown ten years younger, and overflowed with reminiscences of Afghanistan and the Ghazees; while Lieutenant Lawson might, from his high spirits and cheery behaviour, have been just starting on a hunting expedition or some pleasure excursion.

At last it came: "Prepare to mount!"

"Well, here goes!" said Jack, drawing his steed's head round, and putting his foot in the stirrup. "Here goes!" echoed Joe Crouch.

"Mount!" The bugle sounded the advance, the word was given, and the column moved off across the undulating plain—the Guards in front, baggage camels in the centre, and the Mounted Infantry bringing up the rear; the length of the column extending to nearly a mile.

Scared gazelles sprang up from among the rocks and bushes, and bounded away.

"Hi, Swabs! where's yer catapult?" inquired Tommy Briggs.

"Keepin' it for the niggers," answered the marksman significantly.

After an hour's going, many of the riders sought to ease themselves, and vary the peculiar swaying motion by a change of position: some crossed their legs in front of them; while Jack and his chum sat side-saddle, facing each other, and for the twentieth time that day exchanged opinions as to when and where they would first come in touch with the enemy.

In addition to the heat, the clouds of dust raised by the force in front rendered it choky work for those in rear; and no one was sorry when, about five o'clock, the bugles sounded the halt.

Jack dismounted, feeling uncommonly sore and stiff, but was soon busily engaged helping to make fires of dry grass and mimosa scrub, on which to boil the camp kettles for tea.

Never, even when poured from Queen Mab's old silver teapot, had the steaming beverage tasted so refreshing; and the men, sitting round in groups, mess-tin in hand, seemed to regard the whole business in the light of a gigantic picnic. The sun dropped below the horizon; and after a rest of about an hour and a half, the march was continued, the column closing up and proceeding with a broadened front.

The clear, brilliant light of the moon flooded the scene with silvery splendour, throwing up in strange contrast the black, dark hills in the distance. Gradually, as the men grew sleepy, their laughter and conversation died away, the padded feet of the camels made no sound as they passed over the sand, and the silence remained unbroken save for the occasional yelping bark of some hungry jackal. Jack felt cold and drowsy, and, in spite of the movement of his camel, had hard work to keep awake.

Once or twice, when the loads of some of the baggagers slipped, a halt was called while they were refixed; and men, dismounting from their saddles, fell fast asleep on the sand, only to be roused again in what seemed a moment later by the "advance" being sounded.

Hours seemed drawn out into weeks, and Jack, glancing with heavy eyes to his left front, wondered if the sky would ever brighten with the signs of dawn. At length the east grew grey, then flushed with pink, and the sun rose with the red glare of a conflagration, sending a glow of warmth across the desert. For about two hours the march was continued; then, at a spot where a number of trees were growing, a halt was made, camels unloaded, and preparations made for a well-earned breakfast.

In spite of the excitement of this first bivouac, as soon as the meal was over Jack stretched himself out upon the ground and fell fast asleep, only returning to consciousness when wakened by the flies and midday heat; and so ended his first experience of a desert march.

For the purposes of this story it will not be necessary to follow closely all our hero's doings during the next fortnight; and we shall therefore rest content with describing, as briefly as possible, the movements of the force during that period of time which preceded its coming in actual contact with the enemy.

Starting again on the afternoon of the thirty-first of December, the column pushed forward with occasional halts, until, early on the morning of the second of January, Gakdul was reached, and the wells occupied without resistance. Leaving the Guards and Engineers to garrison the place, the rest of the column marched the same evening on the return journey to Korti, to collect and bring on the remaining troops and stores necessary for continuing the advance to Metemmeh. Ten days later, the remainder of the force arrived at Gakdul; and after a day spent in watering and attending to arms and ammunition, a start was made on the afternoon of the fourteenth in the direction of Abu Klea. Soon after sunset the column halted, and resuming the march early on the following morning, by five o'clock in the evening had reached Jebel-es-Sergain, or the Hill of the Saddle, which was to be the resting-place for the night.

The men lay down as usual, with piled arms in front and camels in rear; the order for perfect silence was hardly needed; the sandy water-channels made a comfortable couch for wearied limbs; and the tired warriors were glad enough to wrap themselves in their blankets, and enjoy a few hours of well-earned repose.

In spite of the long and fatiguing day through which he had just passed, Jack did not fall asleep at once, like the majority of his comrades. Ever since his meeting with Valentine, his mind had been continually going back to the days when they were at school together; and now, in the solemn stillness of the desert, as he lay gazing up at the

169

bright, starlit sky, his thoughts flew back to Brenlands, and he pictured up the dear face that had always been the chief of the many attractions that made the place so pleasant. He almost wished now that he had written to her before leaving England. She knew where Valentine was, and every morning would glance with beating heart at the war headings in the newspaper. It would have been a great satisfaction to feel confident of having a share in her loving thoughts. Since Christmas Day, our hero had only caught an occasional glimpse of his cousin, but that was sufficient to revive his old love for the bright, frank-looking face.

"He's just the same as ever," thought Jack. "Well, I hope he'll get through this all right. There are the girls, and Aunt Mabel—it would be dreadful if anything happened!" And with this reflection Fenleigh J. turned over and fell asleep.

Before daybreak next morning the column was once more on the move, crossing a large waste of sand and gravel, relieved here and there by stretches of black rock; while, bordering the plain on either side, were ranges of hills, which gradually approached each other until, in the distance, they formed the pass through which ran the track leading to the wells of Abu Klea.

The march was now beginning to tell upon the camels, which, weakened by fatigue and short allowance of forage, fell down in large numbers through sheer exhaustion, throwing the transport into great confusion.

Shortly before mid-day the force halted at the foot of a steep slope for the usual morning meal of tea and bully beef.

"I shan't be sorry when we get to those wells," said Jack, sipping at the lid of his mess-tin; "I've been parched with thirst ever since we left Gakdul. I wonder it we shall reach them this evening!"

"I don't reckon it's much further," answered Joe Crouch. "I heard the Nineteenth are going on ahead to water their horses. Look! they're just off."

Jack watched the Hussars as they disappeared over the brow of the hill.

"Lucky beggars!" he muttered, and lying down upon his bed he pulled his helmet over his eyes, and prepared for a quiet snooze before the order should be given to mount.

He had been dozing, and was in the dreamy stage between waking and sleeping, when his attention was attracted by a conversation which was taking place in his immediate vicinity. A few yards away, Lieutenant Lawson was sitting on the ground rearranging the folds of his putties, and talking to another subaltern.

"I shouldn't have brought a thing like that with me," the latter was saying; "you might lose it. Any old silver one's good enough for this job, especially if you get bowled over, and some villain picks your pockets."

"Well, I hadn't another," answered Lawson; "and, after all, it didn't cost me much. I knew a fellow at Melchester, called Fosberton, an awful young ass. He got into debt, and was hard pushed to raise the wind. He wanted me to buy this. I was rather sorry for the chap, so I gave him five pounds for it, and told him he could have it back if he chose to refund the money; but he left the town soon after that, and I've never heard from him since. Hallo! What's up now?"

A couple of horsemen were galloping down the slope, and a few minutes later the command was passed back from the front,—

"Fall in! Examine arms and ammunition!"

The men sprang forward to the row of piled arms, and then, like an electric current, the report passed from one to another—the enemy was in sight!

"Cast loose one packet of your ammunition," said the commander of the company.

Jack's fingers twitched with excitement as he pulled off the string of the familiar little brown paper parcel, and dropped the ten cartridges into his pouch. It was the real thing now, and no mistake!

Moving forward in line of columns, the force ascended the slope, and after one more brief halt, while further reconnaissances were being made, began to advance across the level stretch beyond, from which a good view was obtained of the distant valley of Abu Klea, with the steep hills rising on either side, and opening out at the entrance of the pass.

"There they are!"

Far away, on the dark, rocky eminences, crowds of tiny, white-robed figures could be clearly distinguished moving and gesticulating in an excited manner.

Steadily the force advanced until, when within a comparatively short distance of the mouth of the valley, the word for "close order" was given. The camels were driven forward into a solid mass in rear of the leading company as it halted; the men dismounted, and knee-lashed their steeds.

There was not much time for looking about, for the order was immediately given to build a zareba; and while some men were set to work to cut down brushwood, Jack and his comrades were told off to gather stones for constructing a breastwork.

"Look alive, my lads!" said Sergeant Sparks, "and get whatever you can. Hallo!" he added; "they've begun, have they?"

Jack had heard something like the sound of the swift flight of a swallow far overhead, but he did not understand its significance until, a moment later, the sound was repeated, and on the ground in front of him there suddenly appeared a mark, as though some one had struck the sand with the point of an invisible stick, leaving behind a short, deep groove, and causing a handful of dust to spring into the air. Far away on the distant hillside was a tiny puff of smoke, and as he looked the faint pop of the rifle reached his ear. Then the truth dawned on him: this was his baptism of fire—

a long-range fire, to be sure, but none the less deadly if the bullet found its billet!

He caught up a fragment of rock, and carried it to where the wall was to be constructed. Men were hurrying to and fro all around him, and yet suddenly he seemed to feel himself alone, the sole mark for the enemy's fire; again that z—st overhead, and a cold chill ran down his back. He shut his teeth, and, with a careless air, strode off for a fresh load. He had not gone twenty yards when another shot ricochetted off a stone, and flew up into the air with a shrill chirrup. Jack winced and shivered. It was no good, however well he might conceal the fact from others—the fear of death was on him; it was impossible to deceive his own heart. A fresh terror now seized him, coupled with a sense of shame. He was the fellow who had always expressed a wish to be a soldier, and go on active service; and now, before the first feeble spitting of the enemy's fire, all his courage was ebbing away. What if his comrades should notice that his limbs trembled and his voice was shaky? What if, when the advance was made, his nerve should fail him altogether, and he should turn to run?

With dogged energy he pursued his task, hardly noticing what was going on around him. For the fourth time he was approaching the zareba, when a comrade, a dozen yards in front, stumbled forward and sank down upon the ground. There was no cry, no frantic leap into the air, yet it was sufficiently horrible. Jack felt sick, and his teeth chattered; he had never before seen a man hit, and it was his first experience of the sacrifice of human flesh and blood. At the same moment, like a clap of thunder, one of the screw-guns was discharged; the droning whizz of the shell grew fainter and fainter—a pause—and then the boom of its explosion was returned in a muffled echo from the distant hillside.

A couple of men hurried forward and raised their wounded comrade. Jack turned away his eyes, and immediately they encountered a rather different spectacle.

A young subaltern, with a short brier pipe in his mouth, and without a hair on his face, was making a playful pretence of dropping a huge boulder on to the toes of the lieutenant of Jack's detachment.

"Hold the ball—no side!" said Mr. Lawson facetiously. "Look here, Mostyn, you beggar! I've just spotted a fine rock, only it's too big for one to carry. Come and help to bring it in; it's a chance for you to distinguish yourself. Look sharp! or some of the Tommies will have bagged it."

Something in this speech, and the careless, happy-go-lucky way in which it was uttered, seemed to revive Jack's spirits. Mr. Lawson recognized and spoke to him as he passed.

"Well, Fenleigh, they've begun to shake the pepper-box at us; but it'll be our turn to-morrow."

There was nothing in the remark itself, but there was something in the cheery tone and manly face of the speaker; something that brought fresh courage to the soldier's heart, and filled it with a sudden determination to emulate the example of his leader.

"Yes, sir," he answered briskly, and from that moment his fears were banished.

Slowly the construction of the zareba was completed—a low, stone wall in front, and earthen parapets and abattis of mimosa bushes on the other three sides. The enemy still continued a dropping fire, which was replied to with occasional rounds of shrapnel from the guns; but Jack saw no further casualties.

Once, during the work of collecting stones, he encountered Valentine.

"I say," remarked the latter, acknowledging his cousin's salute with a nod and a smile, "this reminds me of the time when we went up the river with the girls to Starncliff, and built up a fireplace to boil the kettle."

When darkness fell, the force was assembled within the zareba; the low breastwork was manned in double rank, every soldier lying down in his fighting place, with belts on, rifle by his side, and bayonet fixed; all lights were extinguished, and talking and smoking forbidden. In spite of the day's exertions, few men felt inclined for sleep; the drumming of tom-toms, and the occasional whistle of a bullet overhead, were not very effective as a lullaby, and served as a constant reminder of the coming struggle.

Jack settled himself into as comfortable a position as his belts and accoutrements would allow, and lay gazing up at the silent, starlit sky. What was death? and what came after? Before another night he himself might know. Lying there in perfect health, it seemed impossible to realize that before another night his life might have ended. He turned his thoughts to Brenlands. Yes; he would like to have said good-bye to Aunt Mabel, and to have had once more the assurance from her own lips that he was still "my own boy Jack!"

"I always make a mess of everything," he said to himself. "I thought I should always have had Brenlands to go to; and first of all I got chucked out of the school a year before I need have left, and then this happens about the watch. In both cases I've Raymond Fosberton to thank, in a great measure, for what happened. I'll pay him out if ever I get the chance."

The thought of his cousin brought back to his mind the recollection of the conversation he had overheard that morning. Strange that Mr. Lawson should have known Raymond! Jack wondered what the monetary transaction could have been that had been alluded to by his officer.

Gradually a sense of drowsiness crept over him, and his heavy head sank back upon the sand.

"Stand to your arms!" He clutched instinctively at the rifle by his side, and rose to his feet; the noise of the tom-toms seemed close at hand.

"They're coming!" But no; it was a false alarm. Once more the men settled down, and silence fell on the zareba. Suddenly there was a wild yell from one of the sleepers.

"What's up there?—man hit?"

"No—silly chump!—only dreaming!"

Again Jack dozed off, to be wakened, after what seemed only a moment of forgetfulness, by Joe Crouch shaking him by the shoulder. The word was once more being passed along, "Stand to your arms!" and the men lay with their hands upon their rifles. Daybreak was near, and an attack might be expected at any moment.

The sky was ghostly with the coming dawn, the air raw and cold. Jack shivered, and "wished for the day."

# CHAPTER XVIII.

## THE BATTLE.

"Then he heard a roaring sound, quite terrible enough to frighten the bravest man."—*The Brave Tin Soldier.*

Numbed with the cold, and stiff from lying so long in a cramped position, Jack and many of his comrades rose as the daylight strengthened, to stretch their legs and stamp some feeling into their feet. As they did so, however, the dropping shots of the enemy rapidly increased to a sharp fusilade; bullets whizzed overhead, or knocked up little spurts of sand and dust within the zareba; and the defenders were glad enough to once more seek the shelter of the low wall and parapet of earth. Several men were wounded, and the surgeons commenced their arduous duties—services which so often demand the exercise of the highest courage and devotion, and yet seldom meet with their due share of recognition in the records of the battlefield. Ever and anon the screw-guns thundered a reply to the popping of the distant rifle fire, and men raised their heads to watch the effect of the shrapnel, as each shot sped away on its deadly errand.

Even amid such surroundings, hunger asserted itself; and breakfast was served out, a good draught of hot tea being specially acceptable after the long exposure to the cold night air.

"When you're on active service, eat and sleep whenever you can," said Sergeant Sparks, munching away at his bully beef and biscuit. "There's never no telling when you'll get another chance."

Bands of the enemy kept appearing and disappearing in the distance; spear-heads and sword-blades flashed and glittered in the rosy morning sunlight, and the tom-toms kept up a continual thunder; but still there was no sign of an attack.

Jack longed to be doing something. He lay on the ground nervously digging pits with his fingers in the soft sand, listening to the monotonous murmur of conversation going on around him, and the constant z—st! z—st! of bullets flying over and into the zareba. Now and again he exchanged a few remarks with "Swabs" or Joe Crouch; and when at length he was told off to join a party of skirmishers, he sprang up and seized his rifle with a sigh of relief.

Moving out in extended order to the right front of the zareba, they marched forward a short distance, then halted, and lay down to fire a volley.

"Ready, at eleven hundred yards. Now, men, be steady, and take your time."

"Swabs" was in his element. He sprawled his legs wide apart, rooted his left elbow into the sand, and settled down as though he were firing for the battalion badge on the range at Melchester. Our hero was not quite so cool; his heart thumped and his fingers twitched as he adjusted the sliding bar of his back-sight.

"Aim low—present—fire!"

The rifles were discharged with a simultaneous crash.

"Good volley," said Mr. Lawson, who was kneeling, peering through his field-glass; "a bit short, I'm afraid; put your sights up to eleven-fifty."

Jack opened the breach of his rifle with a sharp jerk, and drew a long breath. For the life of him he could not have told whether his aim had been good or bad, but this much he knew, that he had fired his first shot in actual conflict.

The skirmishers retired; but still the enemy hung back, too wary to attempt a charge. At length the order was given for an advance, and preparations were accordingly made for forming a moving square. The various detachments marched out of the zareba and lay down as they took up their positions. Camels for carrying the wounded, and conveying water and reserve ammunition, were drawn up in the centre; the two guns and the Gardiner with its crew of sailors taking positions respectively within the front and rear faces of the formation.

Jack raised himself and looked round, anxious, if possible, to make out the whereabouts of his cousin. He could distinguish "Heavies," Blue-jackets, and the Guards, but Valentine and the —sex men were stationed somewhere out of sight on the other side of the central mass of baggagers and their drivers. A short wait, and then came the order,—

"Rise up! The square will advance!"

Two deep, as in the days of the "thin red line," the men marched forward, stumbling over rocky hillocks and deep water-ruts, vainly attempting to keep unbroken their solid formation, and delayed by the slow movement of the guns and camels. The Arabs, swarming on either flank, opened a heavy fire. The flight of the bullets filled the air with a continual buzz. Men dropped right and left, and a halt was made while the wounded were placed on the cacolets. The sides of the square turned· outwards, the Mounted Infantry formed its left-front corner, and Jack and his comrades were in the left face.

"Why can't we give 'em a volley?" murmured "Swabs," gazing at the feathery puffs of smoke on the distant hillside, which looked so innocent, but each of which might mean death to the spectator. No order, however, was given to fire, and the command, "Right turn—forward!" put the marksman and his comrades once more in motion.

To walk along and be shot at was not exactly the ideal warfare of his boyhood: but Jack had been "blooded" by this time, and trudged along with a set face, paying little attention to the leaden hail which swept overhead, and only wishing that something would happen to bring matters to a crisis.

A few minutes later his attention was turned to the line of skirmishers, who were moving, some little distance away, in a direction parallel to the march of the square. Suddenly, close to two of these, a couple of Arabs sprang up from behind some bushes. One rushed upon the nearest Englishman; but the latter parried the spear-thrust, and without a pause drove his bayonet through his adversary's chest. The other native turned and ran.

"Bang! bang!" went a couple of rifle shots; but the fugitive escaped untouched, and disappeared behind the brow of an adjacent knoll.

"See that, Lawson?" inquired a voice from the supernumerary rank.

"Yes," answered the subaltern, "like potting rabbits. I think I could have wiped that fellow's eye if I'd been there. The bayonet *versus* lance was done better."

Jack glanced round, and saw the speaker smoking a pipe, while Sergeant Sparks tramped along close behind with an approving smile upon his face, as though, if questioned, he would have made exactly the same observation himself. It was no time to be fastidious or sentimental; the callous indifference to life and death, whether real or assumed, was the thing wanted. Here, at least, were two superiors who did not seem to consider the situation very serious. The young soldier shifted his rifle to the other shoulder, and grasped the butt with a firmer grip.

For an hour, which might have been a lifetime, the square toiled on, every now and again changing direction to gain more open ground; the stretchers and cacolets constantly receiving fresh burdens. A man, two files in front of our hero, went down with a bullet through the head, and those in rear stumbled over him.

"Close up! close up, and keep that corner blocked in!"

With mouth parched with the stifling heat and dust, Jack sucked at the lukewarm dregs of his water-bottle, and wondered if the river itself would ever quench his thirst. "Swabs," his rear-rank man, kept fingering the loose cartridges in his pouch. At length the marksman's patience and *sang froid* seemed exhausted.

"Is this going on for ever?" he blurted out, "Ain't we ever going to give it 'em back?"

Hardly had the question been asked, when the answer was made evident in a most unmistakable manner.

Away in the grass to the left front a number of white and green flags, mounted on long poles, had been for some time visible; and at this point, as though they sprang out of the ground, swarms of Arabs suddenly made their appearance, and with headlong speed and reckless devotion charged down upon the left-front corner of the square. The scattered line of skirmishers turned and fled for their lives; while behind them, like a devouring tidal wave, the vast black mass rushed forward, their fierce shouts filling the air with a hollow roar like that of a ground sea.

Like many another young soldier, with nothing but a few hundred yards of desert between himself and death, Jack's first impulse was to raise his rifle and blaze away at random as fast as he could load; but the clear, calm voices in the supernumerary rank, and the old habit of discipline, held him in check.

"Steady, men:—Aim low—Fire a volley!"

Another moment, and the black mass with its waving banners and glittering weapons disappeared in a burst of fire and smoke, as the rifles spoke with a simultaneous crash. Again, and yet again, the vivid sheet of flame flashed from the side of the square; then, through the drifting fog, it was seen that the enemy were apparently changing the direction of their attack. Falling in scores before the

"The enemy swerved round the flank of the square, and
burst furiously upon the rear."

terrible, scythe-like sweep of the volley firing, they swerved round the flank of the square and burst furiously upon the rear.

Rapid independent firing had succeeded the regular volleys, and Jack was in the act of using his rifle, when he became conscious of a shock and swaying movement, like the commencement of a Rugby scrimmage. He turned, and saw in a moment what had happened: by sheer weight of numbers, the overpowering rush of Arabs had forced back the thin line of "Heavies," and a fierce hand-to-hand fight was in progress. What had been the interior of the square was now covered with a confused mass of struggling combatants, dimly seen through clouds of dust and smoke. Desperate fanatics hacked and stabbed with their heavy swords and long spears, while burly giants of the Guards returned equally deadly strokes with butt and sword-bayonet. Shouts, cries, and words of command mingled in a general uproar, half-drowned in the incessant din of the firing.

How long this awful contest lasted, or exactly what happened, Jack could never clearly remember. He was conscious that the rear rank had turned about, and of a vision of "Swabs" standing like a man shooting rabbits in a cover, with his rifle at his shoulder, waiting for a chance of a clear shot. Turning again to his front, he noticed the fellow on his right working frantically at his lever, and sobbing with rage and excitement over a jammed cartridge-case. "Knock it out with your cleaning-rod!" he yelled, and thrust another round into the breach of his own weapon, determined, if this were the end, to make a hard fight of the finish.

At length the pressure seemed to grow less, and then ceased; the enemy wavered, then turned and began to slowly retreat, hesitating every now and again, even in face of the withering rifle fire, as though half-minded to renew their attack. Some turned and shook their fists, while others, with the fanatic's unconquerable spirit and reckless valour, rushed back singly, only to fall long before they reached the hated foe.

Once the threatening attitude of the retiring masses raised the cry of "Close up! they're coming again!" But a well-directed volley settled the question, and the last stragglers soon disappeared behind the distant sandhills.

Cheer on cheer rose from the square, and Jack, grounding the butt of his heated weapon, joined in with a right good will, for he had fought his first battle, and his heart throbbed with the triumph of victory.

But even now the conflict was not quite over. Arab marksmen were still lurking in the broken ground, and one of them suddenly rose into view from behind a rock. Levelling his piece he fired, and Mr. Lawson, who, revolver in hand, had stepped into a gap in the ranks, fell forward on his face, the blood gushing in a crimson torrent from his mouth. At the same moment "Greek met Greek;" for "Swabs," throwing his rifle into his shoulder fired, and the Arab sharpshooter tossed up his arms and dropped out of sight behind a rock.

Our hero fell upon his knees with something like a sob, and attempted to raise the fallen man. There was no lack of assistance. Mr. Lawson was one of those officers for whose sake men are always ready and glad to risk their lives; but the boldest among them could do nothing for him now, and a moment or so later he died in Jack's arms.

"He's gone, right enough, poor fellow!" said Captain Hamling, the commander of the company, who had hurried to the spot. "See what's in his pockets, Fenleigh. It there's anything of value, it must be taken care of, and sent to his people."

Jack did as he was ordered. A pipe, tobacco-pouch, jack-knife, and rolled bandage were the chief things he found; and he handed them to the captain. There was still the breast-pocket of the tunic, and this on examination was found to contain a small letter-case and a handsome gold watch. Jack glanced at the timepiece, and very nearly let it drop from his fingers to the ground; he knew it in a moment—the lost treasure which years ago had been stolen from Queen Mab's cupboard. This then was the thing which Raymond Fosberton had parted with for five pounds.


The square moved on a short distance to ground less encumbered with the slain, and then halted. The carnage was awful; dead and dying of the enemy lay in heaps where they had fallen, mown down by the deadly fire of the Martinis; while among them on the knoll where the square had been broken, and in many cases hardly recognizable from the blood and dust which covered their forms and faces, were the bodies of the Englishmen who had perished in the fray.

Orders were now given for burying the dead, collecting the arms and ammunition, and destroying the useless weapons that lay scattered about in all directions; and it was while engaged in this latter duty that Jack encountered his cousin.

"I've just been inquiring for you. Thank God, you're safe!"

In spite of all that he had just passed through, Jack's thoughts were not fixed upon the fighting or dearly-won victory.

"O Val!" he blurted out, "I've found that watch—the one that was stolen at Brenlands!"

In a few hurried sentences he described the conversation he had overheard, and the discovery of the timepiece in the dead lieutenant's pocket. The dread scene around him was for the moment forgotten in his anxiety to clear his character from the doubts which he imagined must still be entertained to a certain extent by his former friend.

"So you see, sir," he concluded, "I can now prove that I'm no thief. Raymond Fosberton stole it. I wish you'd ask

Captain Hamling to show it to you, sir, and then you'd know
I'm speaking the truth."

Valentine listened to this extraordinary revelation in
open-eyed astonishment.

"There's no need for that," he answered—"I'll ask to see it
if it's your particular wish—but, Jack, I wish you would
believe that what I say is true, and that neither I nor Queen
Mab ever for a moment imagined that you were the thief.
You may doubt us, but we have never lost faith in you."

# CHAPTER XIX.

## "FOOD FOR POWDER."

"And so he lay quite still, while the shot rattled through the rushes, and gun after gun was fired over him."—*The Ugly Duckling.*

At last the wells were reached, and after the wants of the wounded had been supplied, Jack and his comrades got a chance of quenching their parching thirst.

Water! It was a moving sight—a crowd of men standing round a pit, at the bottom of which appeared a little puddle, which when emptied out would gradually drain in again, the spectators watching its progress with greedy eyes. Never had "Duster's" celebrated home-made ginger-beer tasted so refreshing as this muddy liquid. Jack sighed in an ecstasy of enjoyment as he gulped it down, and Joe Crouch remarked that he wished his throat was as long as a "hostridge's."

A body of three hundred men from the Guards, Heavies, and Mounted Infantry started on a return journey to the zareba to bring up the baggage, and the remainder of the force bivouacked near the wells. The night was fearfully cold; the men had nothing but the thin serge jumpers which they had worn during the heat of the day to protect them against the bitter night air. Shivering and gnawed with hunger, Jack, Joe Crouch, "Swabs," and two more men huddled together in a heap; and finding it impossible to sleep, endeavoured to stay the cravings of their empty stomachs with an occasional whiff of tobacco, those who were without pipes obtaining the loan of one from a more fortunate comrade. Jack's thoughts wandered back to Brenlands, and he smiled grimly to himself at the recollection of that first camping-out experience, and of Queen Mab's words as she promised them a supply of rugs

and cushions, "Perhaps some day you won't be so well off."
His mind was still full of his recent discovery. The thought
that his friends must regard him as guilty of the theft, and the
feeling that he could never give them proof to the contrary,
had rankled in his heart more, perhaps, than he himself
suspected; and now that he had at last discovered a solution
to the riddle, and could prove beyond the possibility of a
doubt who was the guilty party, he longed to ease his soul by
talking the matter over with some one who knew the
circumstances of the case. Joe Crouch was the very man.

"Joe."

"Yes."

"You remember my cousin, Raymond Fosberton?"

Joe was not in the best of humours; he was cold, and his
pipe had gone out.

"Yes, I do," he grumbled. "I wish I had him here now in
his white weskit and them shiny boots!" The speaker drew
hard at his empty clay, which gave forth a fierce croak, as
though it thoroughly approved of its owner's sentiments.

"D'you remember that time when the watch was stolen
out of Miss Fenleigh's cupboard?"

"Yes; and that Fosberton said it might 'a been me as
took it, and Master Valentine told me afterwards that you
said that though I'd stolen some pears once, you knew I was
honest. Ay, but I thought of that the morning I seen you
come into the barrack-room. And then he told them as it
was you 'ad done it. My eye! if I had him here now, I'd
knock his face out through the back of his head!" The clay
pipe literally crowed with rage.

"Well, you may be interested to hear that it was
Raymond Fosberton himself who took the watch." And Jack
proceeded to tell the story of his find.

"So he stole it himself, did he?" exclaimed Crouch, as
the narrative concluded. "Law me! if I had him here, I'd—"

"Never mind!" interrupted the other, laughing. "I may
have a chance of settling up with him myself some day."

"What shall you do when you see him?"

"Oh, I don't know!" answered Jack. "I daresay I shall have my revenge."

Joe relapsed into silence, but for some time sudden squeaks from his pipe showed that he was still meditating on the terrible vengeance which he would mete out to Raymond Fosberton, should that gentleman leave his comfortable lodgings in England and appear unexpectedly in the Bayuda Desert.

At length the morning came, and with it the report that the baggage-train was in sight. The news was welcome, and the work of knee-lashing and unloading the camels did not take long. The previous morning's hasty breakfast under fire had not been, by any means, a satisfying meal; and so, after a fast of nearly two days, the prospect of food made the men active enough in unpacking the stores.

Jack seized his ration of bully beef and biscuit with the fierce eagerness of a famished wolf; cold, hunger, and weary, sleepless nights had never been the lot of the lead troops campaigning on the lumber-room floor at Brenlands, or of their commanders either; nor, for the matter of that, is it usual for youthful, would-be warriors to associate such things with the triumph of a victory.

Our hero had finished his meal, and was cleaning his rifle, when he was accosted by Joe Crouch.

"I say, Mr. Fenleigh wants to see you. He's over there by the guns."

Valentine was standing talking to some of his fellow-officers. He turned away from the group as he saw his cousin approaching, and the latter halted and accorded him the customary salute.

"Look here," said the subaltern, "the general is sending dispatches back to Korti, and the officers have the opportunity of telegraphing to their friends in England. I'm going to send a message home to let them know I'm all right. Shall I put in a word for you? I'm sure," added the speaker, "that Aunt Mabel would be glad to know that you are here, and quite safe and sound after the fighting."

Jack hesitated, but there was no sign yet of the long lane turning.

"It's very good of you, sir," he answered, "but I'd rather they didn't know my whereabouts. If I live through this, and return to England, I shall still be a private soldier. I'm much obliged to you, sir, all the same."

He saluted again, and walked away. Valentine looked after the retreating figure with a queer, sad smile upon his face.

"You're a difficult fish to deal with," he muttered; "but we shall land you again some day, though I hardly know how."

Late in the afternoon the column was once more in motion, and then commenced an experience which Jack, and all those who shared in it, have probably never forgotten. At first the march was orderly, but, as the hours went by, progress became more and more difficult. Camels, half-starved and exhausted, lagged and fell, causing continual delay and confusion. The desert track having been abandoned in order to avoid possible collision with the enemy, the road lay at one time through a jungle of mimosa trees and bushes, when the disorder was increased tenfold—baggagers slipped their loads, and ranks opening out to avoid obstacles found it impossible in the dark to regain their original formation. Utterly unable to keep awake, men fell asleep as they rode, drifting out of their places, some, indeed, straying off into the darkness, never to be seen again.

Worn out, and chilled to the bone with the bitter night air, Jack clung to his saddle, dozing and waking; dreaming for an instant that Queen Mab was speaking to him, and rousing with a start as the word was passed, "Halt in front!" to allow time for the rear-guard closing up with the stragglers. At each of these pauses poor "Lamentations" knelt of his own accord; and his rider, dropping down on the sand by his side, fell into a deep sleep, to be awakened by the complaining grunts of the camels as the word, "All right in rear!" gave the signal for a fresh start.

After each stoppage it was no easy matter to get the weary animals on their legs again; and almost equally difficult in many instances to rouse their riders from the heavy slumber into which they fell the moment they stretched themselves upon the ground.

"Pass the word on, 'All right in rear!'"

"Oh, dear! I'd give a month's pay for an hour's sleep," mumbled Joe Crouch.

"Get up, you fool!" answered Jack, kicking the recumbent figure of his comrade. "D'you want to be left behind?"

On, on, through the endless darkness, now for a moment unconscious, now half awake, but always with the sense of being cold and weary, the long night march seemed to last a lifetime. Then, as sometimes happens in similar circumstances, a half-forgotten tune took possession of his tired brain, the once familiar melody of Queen Mab's hymn; and in a dreamy fashion he kept humming it over and over again, sometimes the air alone, and sometimes with snatches of the words, as they came back to his memory.
"Rest comes at length;......
The day must dawn, and darksome night be past."

His head sank forward on his breast. It was Sunday evening at Brenlands, and Helen was playing the piano. Queen Mab was standing close at his side; and yet, somehow, the whole world lay between them. "You may doubt us, but we have never lost faith in you." He turned to see who spoke, and the figures in his dream vanished, leaving only the echo of their voices in his mind.
"......Angels of light!
Singing to welcome the pilgrims of the night!"

The tune was still droning in his head when the first grey streaks of dawn gave warning of the approaching day, and, in the growing light, the column gradually regained its proper formation.

The line of march lay down a vast slope covered with grass and shrubs, which stretched away towards the distant Nile, as yet out of sight; and ere long word was received from the cavalry scouts that the enemy, in large numbers, were close at hand.

Once more the bullets of the sharpshooters whistled overhead; and the Arabs appearing in considerable force on the left flank, the column was halted on the summit of a low knoll, and orders were issued for the construction of a zareba.

All hands now set to work to unload the camels and build walls of saddles, biscuit-boxes, and other stores— parapets formed of almost as incongruous materials as the old domino and pocket-knife works behind which the lead warriors took shelter at Brenlands. Skirmishers were thrown out to keep down the enemy's fire; but the men were worn out, and having nothing to aim at but the feathery puffs of smoke rising amidst the distant grass and bushes, they failed to dislodge the Arab marksmen.

Jack and his comrades "lay low," glad to avail themselves of the shelter afforded by the side of the zareba. The bullets whizzed overhead, or struck the biscuit-boxes with a sharp smack, while some dropped with a sickening thud into the mass of camels. They were patient sufferers, and even when struck made no sound or attempt to move. Stretchers being constantly carried to and fro showed that the medical staff had plenty of work; but it was not until some hours later that the news leaked out among the men that Sir Herbert Stewart himself was mortally wounded.

Feeling inclined for a smoke, and having no tobacco about him, our hero asked permission to fetch a supply from the zuleetah-bag attached to his saddle. "Lamentations" acknowledged his approach with the usual grumble; but it was the last greeting he was ever destined to give his master. A bullet flew past with a sharp zip, the poor beast started and shivered, and a thin stream of blood trickled down his shoulder. Poor "Lam!" he was unclean and unsavoury, an inveterate grumbler, and possessed apparently of a chronic cold in his nose; his temper was none of the best—he had kicked, and on one occasion had attempted to bite, he had fought his comrades in the lines, and had got the picketing ropes into dire confusion; but, for all that, he was a living thing, and Jack, who was fond of all dumb creatures, watched him with tears in his eyes. It did not last long: the unshapely head sank lower and lower; then suddenly turning his long neck round to the side of his body, the animal rolled over, and all that remained of poor "Lamentations" was a meagre meal for the jackals and vultures.

Hour after hour the men waited, huddled together behind the hastily-formed breastwork of the zareba. "Swabs" occasionally peered through a loophole in the boxes to get a snap-shot at any figure that might be seen creeping about among the distant bushes. Jack, worn out with the night march, stretched himself upon the sand, and, in spite of the constant zip of bullets and discharge of rifles, sank into a deep slumber.

At length he was awakened by a general movement among his comrades: orders had been issued for a portion of the column to fight its way to the Nile, and a square was being formed for the purpose a little to the left of the zareba. In silence, and with anxious expressions on their faces, the men fell into their places, lying down to escape the leaden hail. The force seemed a ridiculously small one to oppose to the swarming masses of the enemy, yet on its success depended the safety of the whole column.

The bugle sounded, and the men sprang to their feet, to be exposed immediately to a heavy fire. Slowly and doggedly they moved forward, now halting to close up gaps, and now changing direction to gain more open ground. The vicious bang of rifles, fired at comparatively close range, told of innumerable sharpshooters lurking around in the grass and shrubs. A bullet suddenly tore the metal ornament from the top of Jack's helmet, and striking the sword-bayonet of a man behind, knocked his rifle nearly out of his hands.

"A miss is as good as a mile!" remarked Sergeant Sparks; but as he spoke Joe Crouch was suddenly flung to the ground as though felled by the stroke of a hammer.

Jack involuntarily uttered a cry of dismay, and the sergeant dropped down on one knee to assist the fallen man. To every one's astonishment, however, the latter rose to his feet unaided, looking rather dazed and gasping for breath, and picking up his rifle staggered back into the ranks. A spent shot had struck him on the bandoleer, demolishing one of the cartridges, but fortunately failing to penetrate the leather belt.

Now and again the square halted to send a volley wherever the enemy seemed to be gathered in any numbers, then continuing the advance in the same cool, deliberate manner.

Jack was marching in the left side, close to one of the rear corners, and, as fate would have it, the left half of the rear face was formed of the ——sex, and from the first he had been close to Valentine. They were within a dozen yards of each other, and every few moments Jack turned his head to assure himself that his cousin was unhurt.

For more than an hour the little square had been doggedly pursuing its forward movement, and now the enemy were seen in black masses on the low hills to the left front.

"They're coming, that's my belief!" said Joe Crouch, turning to address his chum. He got no reply; for, at that instant, as the other happened to look round, he saw his cousin stagger and sink down upon the sand. In an instant

Jack had sprung to his assistance; but this time it was no false alarm. The bullet had done too well its cruel work. For a moment Valentine seemed to recognize him, and looking up, with his left hand still clutching at his breast, made a ghastly attempt to smile. Then, with a groan, he fell over on his side, and fainted.

A stretcher was brought, and Jack was ordered sharply to get back to the ranks. As he took his place the square halted, and an excited murmur rose on all sides:—

"Here they come!—Thank God! they're going to charge!"

# CHAPTER XX.

## THE RIVER'S BRINK.

"Then he could see that the bright colours were faded from his uniform; but whether they had been washed off during his journey, or from the effects of his sorrow, no one could say."—*The Brave Tin Soldier.*

Darkness had fallen, and a thick mist rising from the river made the still, night air damp and penetrating; but the weary men, stretched out upon the sand, slept soundly in spite of the cold, and of the scanty protection from it afforded by their clothing. The dark figures of the sentries surrounding the bivouac, moving slowly to and fro, or pausing to rest on their arms, seemed the only signs of wakefulness, except where the occasional gleam of a lantern shone out as the surgeons went their rounds among the wounded.

Jack, however, was not asleep. He seemed instead to be just waking up from a troubled dream, in which all that had happened since he had seen Valentine placed upon the stretcher had passed before his mind in a confused jumble of sights and sounds, leaving only a vague recollection of what had really taken place:—The oncoming mass of Arabs; the crash of the volleys, changing into the continuous roar of independent firing; the pungent reek of the powder as the rolling clouds of smoke enveloped the square; and the sight of the enemy falling in scores, wavering, slackening the pace of their advance, and finally retreating over the distant hills, not one having reached the line of bayonets. Then, in the growing dusk, as the square advanced, the sight of the silver stream showing every now and again amidst the green, cultivated strip of land upon its banks; the wild joy of men suffering the tortures of a burning thirst, which swelled their tongues and blackened their lips; and the pitiful sight of the wounded being held up that they might catch a glimpse of the distant river; the wait on the brink of the broad stretch of cool, priceless water, as each face of the square moved up in turn to take its fill; and then, no sucking the dregs of a warm water-bottle, but a long, cold, satisfying drink.

All this, though so recently enacted, seemed to have left but a faint impression of its reality on Jack's mind; his one absorbing thought being that Valentine was hit, badly wounded, perhaps dying, or even dead.

A man approached, and in the darkness stumbled over one of the slumberers.

"Now, then, where are you coming to?"

"Dunno—wish I did. D'you men belong to the Blankshire? Where's your officer?"

"Can't say. Wait a minute; that's he lying by that bit of bush—Captain Hamling."

Our hero raised himself into a sitting posture. He had recognized the new-comer as a hospital orderly, and in the surrounding stillness heard him deliver his message:—

"Surgeon Gaylard sends his compliments, and would you allow one of your men named Fenleigh to come and see an officer who's badly wounded? He's some relative I think, sir."

"Very good," answered the captain drowsily; "you can find him yourself."

The orderly had no difficulty in doing that, for in a moment Jack was at his side.

"Is he dying?"

"The oncoming mass of Arabs."

"Dunno; he's badly hurt—shot through the lungs, and he's asked for you several times."

It was a cruel night for the wounded, with nothing to shelter them from the bitter cold. Valentine lay upon the ground, with his head propped up against a saddle. The surgeon was stooping over him as the two men approached, and the light of his lamp tell on the pale, pinched features of the sufferer. Within the last three days Jack had seen scores of men hurried into eternity, and his senses had become hardened by constant association with bloodshed and violent death, yet the sight of those unmistakable lines on that one familiar face turned his heart to stone.

"You're some relative, I believe. He seemed very anxious to see you, so I sent the orderly. What?— Yes, you may stay with him if you like; but keep quiet, and don't let him talk more than you can help."

"Is—is he dying, sir?"

"He may live till morning, but I doubt if he will."

Jack went down on his knees. There was no "sir" this time—sword, and sash, and shoulder-strap were all forgotten.

"Val!" The great, grey eyes, already heavy with the sleep of death, opened wide.

"Jack! my dear Jack!"

"Yes; I've come to look after you. Are you in much pain?"

"No—only when I cough—and—it's dreadfully cold."

The listener stifled down a groan. Ah, dear thoughts of long ago! Such things had never happened on the mimic battlefields at Brenlands. This, then, was the reality.

"Jack, I want you to promise me something—your word of honour to a dying man."

A fit of coughing, ending in a groan of agony, interrupted the request.

"Don't talk too much," answered the other in a broken voice. "What is it you want? I'll do anything for you, God knows!"

"I want you to promise that you'll take this ring to Queen Mab—and give it to her with your own hands. Say that I remembered her always—and carried my love for her with me down into the grave. Promise me that you will give it her—*yourself*!"

Valentine ceased speaking, exhausted with the effort.

"I will, I will!" returned the other, taking the ring. "But don't talk about dying, Val; you'll pull through right enough."

The sufferer answered with a feeble shake of his head, and another terrible fit of coughing left him faint and gasping for breath.

"Stay with me," he whispered.

Jack propped him up to ease his breathing, and wiped the blood from his pallid lips. For a long, long time he sat silently holding the hand of his dying friend; then, fight against it as he would, exhausted nature began to assert herself in an overpowering desire to sleep. Numbed with cold, and wellnigh heart-broken, wretched in body and mind, jealous of the moments as they flew past and of the lessening opportunity of proving his love by any trifling service it might be in his power to render—in spite of all this, an irresistible drowsiness crept over him, and his head fell forward on his knees.

The feeble voice was speaking again.

"What did you say, Val? God forgive me, I cannot keep awake."

Bending close down to catch the words, he could distinguish, even in the darkness, some faint traces of the old familiar smile.

"You used to say—that I had all the luck—but, you remember—at Brenlands—it was the lead captain that got killed."

Jack murmured some reply, he was too worn out and miserable to weep. Once more that terrible struggle to keep his heavy eyes from closing; a dozen times he straightened his back, and groaned in bitterness of spirit at the thought that he could wish to sleep at such a time as this; then once again his head sank under the heavy weight of fatigue and want of rest, and everything became a blank.

Awakening with a start, Jack scrambled to his feet. How long he had slept he could not tell, nor did he realize where he was till the light of a lantern flashing in his eyes brought him to his senses.

"How is—" the question died on his lips.

The surgeon took one keen glance, held the lamp closer, and then raised it again.

"Is he going, sir?"

"Going? he's gone!"

The words were followed by an awful silence; then, for an instant, the yellow gleam of the lamp tell upon the soldier's face.

"Come, come, my lad!" said the medical officer kindly, "we did what we could for him, but it was hopeless from the first. Be thankful that you've got a whole skin yourself. You'd better rejoin your company."

The sky was paling with the first indications of the coming dawn. The men were standing to their arms, and Jack hurried away to take his place in the ranks, hiding his grief as best he could from the eyes of his comrades. Then as he turned to look once more towards the spot whence he had come, he saw, away across the river, the flush of rosy light brighten in the east, and all unbidden there came back to his memory the words of Queen Mab's hymn. The sun rose with a red glare, scattering the mist and sending a glow of warmth across the desert; and once more the old, sweet melody was sounding in his heart, while all around seemed telling of hopes fulfilled and sorrows vanquished when

"Morning's joy shall end the night of weeping."

# CHAPTER XXI.

## "WHEN JOHNNY COMES MARCHING HOME AGAIN!"

*"It touched the tin soldier so much to see her that he almost wept tin tears, but he kept them back. He looked at her, and they both remained silent."—The Brave Tin Soldier.*

It was a hot, still afternoon in August. The birds were silent, hardly a leaf stirred, and everything seemed to have dozed off to sleep in the quiet sunshine. Old Ned Brown, the cobbler, and general "handy-man" of the village, who, in days gone by, had often bound bats and done other odd jobs for "Miss Fenleigh's young nevies," laid down his awl, and gazed out of the window of his dingy little shop.

A soldier was walking slowly down the road. His boots were covered with dust, and on the breast of his red coat glittered the Egyptian medal and the Khedive's Cross.

"That must be Widow Crouch's son," said Ned to himself. "I heard he was back from the war. Maybe he'll know summat about the young gen'leman who used to come and stay up at the house yonder, and who, they say, was killed. Ah, yes! I remember him well—a nice, pleasant-spoken young chap! Dear me, dear me! sad work, sad work!" With a shake of his head, the old man once more picked up the shoe he was mending, still muttering to himself, "Yes, I remember him—sad work, sad work!"

The soldier strode on. His thoughts also were busy with memories of the past. In one sense he was not alone; for before him, in fancy, walked a boy—a rather surly, uncared-for looking young dog, with hands in his pockets, coat thrown open, and Cricket cap perched on the back of his head, as though in open defiance of the rain that was falling. The road had been damp and dismal then; to-day it was dry and dusty; but the heart of the man who trod it was no lighter than it had been that evening ten years ago.

The old cobbler had been mistaken. It was not Joe Crouch, but Jack Fenleigh, who had just passed the window of the little shop. He was thinking of the first time he had come to Brenlands at the commencement of the summer holidays, after having been kept back on the breaking-up day as a punishment for sending a pillow through the glass ventilator of the Long Dormitory.

"I didn't want to face her then," he said to himself, switching the dust off his trousers with his cane. "And yet, how kind she was! Never mind! she won't know me now. Valentine promised he wouldn't write, and he never broke his word."

Jack had walked from Melchester. More than once in the course of the journey he had hesitated, and thought of turning back; but the sacredness of the promise made to a dying man had compelled him to go forward.

He turned the corner, and slackened his pace as he saw before him the old house nestling among the trees. There was no board with TO LET printed on it, such as usually, in story-books, greets the eye of the returning wanderer. The place was just the same as it always had been; and the very fact of its being unchanged appealed to his feelings in a manner which it would be impossible to describe. The white front gate, whose hinges had been so often tried by its being transformed into a sort of merry-go-round; the clumps of laurel bushes which had afforded such good hiding-places in games of "I spy;" even the long-suffering little brass weathercock above the stable roof, which had served as a mark for catapult shooting,—these, and a hundred other objects on which his eyes rested, recalled memories which softened his heart, and brought back more vividly than ever the recollection of that faithful friend, whose last request he was about to fulfil.

"I must do it," he muttered, feeling in his pocket for the ring; "I promised him I would."

He pushed open the gate, and walked almost on tiptoe down the path, casting anxious glances at the windows. To his great relief it was not Jane who opened the door, but a new servant.

"Is Miss Fenleigh in?" he stammered. "Will you tell her a—a private soldier has brought her something from an officer who died in Egypt?"

The girl showed him into the old, quiet parlour (as if he could not have found the way thither himself), and there left him. It was very still. Nothing broke the silence but the sleepy tick of the clock, and the sound of some one (Jakes, perhaps) raking gravel on the garden path. Everything was unaltered. There was the little bust of Minerva that Barbara had once adorned with a paper bonnet; the fretsaw bookcase that the two boys had made at school; and the quaint little glass-fronted cupboard, let into the panelling, from which the watch had been stolen. In the years that had passed, only one thing in the room had changed, and that was the tall figure in uniform standing on the hearthrug.

He turned to look at himself in the glass. The dark moustache, bronzed skin, red tunic with its white collar and badges of the "royal tiger;" all these things had never been reflected there before, and for the twentieth time during the last half-hour he sought to reassure himself with the thought that his disguise was complete. "She'll never recognize me!" he muttered. "It's all right." Then the door opened, and for an instant his heart seemed to stop beating.

The same easy dignity and graciousness of manner, the same sweet womanly face, and the same depths of love and ready sympathy in her clear, calm eyes. She was dressed in mourning, and at her throat was the brooch containing the locks of the children's hair. Jack noticed it at once, and saw, too, that the little silver locket still had its place among the gold trinkets on her watch chain; and the sight of it very nearly brought him down upon his knees at her feet.

She seemed smaller than ever, and now, standing in front of him, her upturned face was about on a level with the medals on his breast.

What was it made his chest heave and his lips tremble as he encountered her gaze? However foolish and headstrong he might have been in the past, he knew he had only to declare himself and it would all be forgotten and forgiven. "You may doubt us," Valentine had said, "but we have never lost faith in you." Yes, that was it; she loved her ugly duckling, believing even now that, in spite of outward appearances, it would one day turn into a swan. But the years had slipped away, and the change had never taken place. She might hope that it had, and it was best that she should never know the truth.

With a set face he began to speak.

"I've lately returned from Egypt, and saw there your nephew, Lieutenant Fenleigh, of the ——sex Regiment."

He tried to say "ma'am," but even at that moment it seemed too great a mockery, and the word choked him.

"I was with him when he died on the banks of the Nile. He asked me to bring you this, and to give it to you with my own hands."

She took the ring, but without moving her eyes from the speaker's face.

"He asked me to tell you that he remembered you always."

The voice grew husky, and the lady drew a little closer, perhaps to hear more plainly what was said.

"And to say that he carried his—his love for you with him down into the grave."

With a great effort Jack finished the message. The words had brought back a flood of vivid recollections of that dreadful night, and his eyes were filled with blinding tears.

He turned to brush them away, and as he did so he felt Queen Mab's arms meet round his neck.

"You dear old boy! don't you think I know you? Don't you think I knew you as soon as you came inside the gate?"

He made some attempt to reply, uttered a broken word or two, and then turned away his head; but she, standing on tiptoe, drew it down lower and lower, until at length it rested on her shoulder.

And so the ugly duckling ended his wanderings.

No autumn frosts or winter snows could ever have fallen on that garden, for here were the same flowers, and fruit, and ferns as had bloomed and ripened that last August holiday seven years ago. So, at least, thought Jack, as he and his aunt walked together along the paths.

"Did he write from Egypt to tell you about me?"

"No; but I've always been expecting you. I knew you'd come back some time."

"I didn't think you'd recognize me."

"Valentine knew I should. Don't you see it was you he sent home to me, and not the ring?"

Jack was silent. Everything that his eye rested upon reminded him of that faithful, boyish friendship, and his lip quivered.

Queen Mab noticed it, and changed the subject.

"I wonder what Jakes will think to see me walking about arm-in-arm with a soldier," she said gaily. "Never mind, I must make the most of it while it lasts. I'm afraid I shan't have many more opportunities of 'keeping company' with a red-coat."

"How d'you mean?" he asked, with an uneasy, downward glance at his uniform. "My time isn't up for nearly three years; and I know I ought not to come here in this rig-out."

"Don't talk nonsense," she answered. "You're a pretty soldier to be ashamed of your cloth. Isn't it possible for a man to do his duty unless he has a pair of epaulettes on his shoulders? Can't he do it under any kind of coat? Come now," she added, shaking his arm, and looking up into his face with a mischievous twinkle in her eyes, "don't you think, for the matter of that, a man could be a hero in his shirt sleeves?"

"Yes," answered Jack, laughing.

"Oh, you do! I'm glad you've come to that conclusion at last."

"Why?"

"Why? because I think you'll soon have to give us a practical illustration of how a man can distinguish himself by being capable and trustworthy, even in plain clothes. That opens up a subject that I have a lot to tell you about. Have you heard that your father and your Uncle John are friends again?"

"Yes; Val said something about it."

"You haven't heard," she continued quietly, "that before the second battle Valentine made a will, and gave it to a friend to be sent home in case he was killed. It was more in the form of a long letter, roughly written on the leaves of a pocket-book. A great deal of it was about you. He did not break his promise to you, and say actually that he had seen you, and where you were; but he assured us that he knew you had not gone to the bad, but were living an honest life, and that before long we should see you again. Then he begged his father, as a last request, to do something for you, and to treat you as his own son. Your uncle was over the other day. He is very anxious to carry out Valentine's wishes, and would like to take you into his own business, with a view to an ultimate partnership."

"It's awfully good of him," murmured Jack huskily.

"Well, that's what he intends to do. But come, it's time I put in the tea."

"It's time I went," he murmured.

"Time you went? What nonsense! You say you've got a week's furlough, and that you left your things at the Black Horse. Well, I'm just going to send Jakes to fetch them. Why, I quite forgot to tell you that little Bar was staying here."

The person who had just stepped out from the open French window on to the lawn was certainly no longer little, but a tall, graceful young lady. There was, however, still some trace in her roguish mouth and dancing eyes of the smaller Barbara who had wrought such havoc among her enemies by firing six peas at a time instead of two.

Jack had never before been frightened at Bar, of all people in the world; but now, if Queen Mab had not still retained her hold of his arm, he might very likely have bolted into the shrubbery.

The girl advanced slowly across the lawn, casting inquiring glances, first at the red coat and medals, and then at the bronzed face of the stranger. Then suddenly her mouth opened, and she quickened her pace to a run.

"Oh, you rascal!" she cried. "It's Jack!"

That was all the speech-making Barbara thought necessary in welcoming the returning prodigal; and not caring a straw for bars and ribbons, pipeclay, and "royal tigers," she embraced him in the same hearty manner as she had always done when they met at the commencement of bygone summer holidays.

The dainty tea-table was a great change after the barrack-room. The pretty china cups seemed wonderfully small and fragile compared with the familiar basin; and once Jack found himself absent-mindedly stuffing his serviette into his sleeve, under the impression that it was his handkerchief.

"Why, when was the last time you had tea here?" asked Barbara. "It must have been that summer when Raymond—" She stopped short, but the last word instantly brought to Jack's mind the recollection of that evening when Fosberton had charged him with being a thief.

"By-the-bye," he exclaimed, "I forgot to tell you—I've found the watch."

"Yes, I know," answered Queen Mab quietly. "Valentine gave a full account of it in his letter."

Jack was just going to launch out into a long and forcible tirade on the subject of the theft, but his cousin signed to him across the table to let the matter drop.

"Aunt has been in such a dreadful way about it," she explained afterwards. "Only she and ourselves know about it. She doesn't like even to have Raymond's name mentioned. He has turned out a thorough scamp, and has given Uncle Fosberton no end of trouble. Father happened to know the friends of that officer who was killed, and when his things were sent home the watch was returned; so it's back again now in the same old place. Aunt has never told any one, not even Raymond himself, as she doesn't want to bring fresh trouble on his parents."

Later on in the evening, as they sat together in the old, panelled parlour in the soft light of the shaded lamp, the talk turned naturally and sweetly on Valentine—on all that he used to say and do; and Jack told as best he could the story of the desert march, and of that last sad parting on the river's brink. After he had finished, there was a silence; then Barbara picked up the piece of work she had laid down.

"So you didn't find war quite such a jolly thing as you used to think it would be?" she said, looking across at him with a tearful smile.

"No," he answered thoughtfully. "I suppose things that you have long set your mind on seldom turn out exactly what you want and expect them to be. I'm glad I saw active service, and I'd go through it all again a hundred times for the sake of having been with Valentine when he died; though it was little I could do for him, more than to say good-bye."

Queen Mab rose from her chair, and stooped over the speaker to wish him good-night.

"Never mind," she said softly. "I'm glad to think of both my boys that their warfare is accomplished!"

# CHAPTER XXII

## CONCLUSION.

"I never dreamed of such happiness as this while I was an ugly duckling!"—*The Ugly Duckling*.

The old house at Brenlands still remains unaltered, except that the empty room upstairs, once the scene of so many terrible conflicts between miniature metal armies, has been turned into a nursery. Another generation of children is growing up now, and eagerly they listen while Aunt Mabel tells the old story of the tin soldier who went adventuring in a paper boat, and came back in the end to the place from which he had started; or the history of the little lead captain, who stands keeping guard over the precious things in the treasure cupboard; and who once, after bearing the brunt of a long engagement, fell in front of his men, just as the fighting ended.

When the nursery is in use, a long-forgotten little gateway makes its appearance at the top of the stairs, and "Uncle Jack" pays toll through the bars to the chubby little Helen standing on the other side.

Queen Mab tries to make out that she is growing older; but her courtiers will not believe it, and go so far as to scoff at and hide her spectacle case, declaring that her wearing glasses is only a pretence.

But though Brenlands and its queen may seem the same as ever, many of those connected with it in our story have experienced changes, of which some mention should be made.

Old Jakes has been obliged to give up the gardening, and Joe Crouch has been installed in his stead. Joe has finished his time, both with the colours and in the reserve; but he is the soldier still—smart, clean, and never needing to

211

have an order repeated twice. He often unconsciously falls back into former habits, and comes marching up the path with his spade at the "slope" or his hoe at the "trail," whistling softly the old quick-step, which once drew our hero to "go with the rest, and follow the drum."

For Jack he cherishes the fondest regard and deepest admiration, which he never hesitates to express in such words as these:—

"Aw, yes, sir! he's what I call the right sort, is Master Jack. He don't turn his back on an old cumred, as some would. I 'member the day he bought himself out. 'Well, good-bye,' says I—'we've been soldierin' together a good time, and in some queer places; but now you're goin' back to be a gen'leman again, and I suppose we shan't see each other never no more.' 'I should be a precious poor gen'leman if I ever forgot you, Joe,' says he; 'you stood by me when I first came to barracks, and some day I hope I shall be able to do something for you in return.' And so he did, for he kept writin' to me, and when my time was up he got me this place. Look here, sir, the day he come to enlist the corporal at the gate says to him, 'We ought to make a general of such a fine chap as you;' and you take my word for it, that's just what they would have made of him, if he'd only stopped long enough!"

Of Barbara something might be said, but that something is for the present supposed to be a secret. Jack, who, like the average boy, always seemed to have a knack of finding out things that were intended to be kept private, knows more than he ought about this matter; and bringing out a handful of coppers at the table, and representing them to be the whole of his savings, declares that he will be "dead broke" should any unforeseen circumstance necessitate his purchasing a wedding present. Whereupon his cousin blushes, and puts her fingers in her ears, and says, "I can't hear," but listens all the time.

Of Raymond Fosberton, perhaps the less said the better. His name has come very near being mentioned in a court of law, for forging his father's signature to a cheque, and is therefore seldom mentioned among his friends. One thing, however, might be told concerning his last visit to Brenlands.

A year after that eventful Christmas in Egypt, Jack was sitting before the fire in Queen Mab's parlour, when Raymond was announced, and shown into the room. He was dressed, as usual, in good though rather flashy clothes; but in spite of this, he looked cheap and common, and his general appearance gave one the impression of dirt wrapped up in silver paper. The moment he saw Jack a spiteful look came into his face, and he took no pains to conceal the old dislike and hatred with which he still regarded the latter.

"Hallo! so you've turned up again. I thought you'd soon get sick of soldiering; too much hard work to suit your book, I expect."

"No; I left it because I had a chance of something better. Aunt Mabel's out; will you wait till she comes back?"

Jack had seen more of the world since the day when he had knocked the visitor into the laurel bush; and could now realize that Queen Mab had spoken the truth when she said that punching heads was not always the most satisfactory kind of revenge. He had a score to settle with Raymond; but he regarded the latter now as a pitiful fellow not worth quarrelling with, and he hesitated, half-minded to let the matter drop without mentioning what was on his mind.

Fosberton mistook the meaning of the other's averted glance. He thought himself master of the situation, and, like a fool, having, figuratively speaking, been given enough rope, he promptly proceeded to hang himself.

"You've been lying low for a precious long time," he continued, maliciously. "Why didn't you come here before? You've been asked often enough!"

"I had my own reasons for stopping away."

"You didn't like to come back after the bother about that watch, I suppose?"

Jack let him run on. "That was partly it," he answered.

"Well, then," continued Raymond, with a sneer, "you made a great mistake bolting like that; you gave yourself away completely."

"I don't understand you," returned the other, with a sharper ring in his voice. "D'you mean to charge me again with having stolen the watch?"

"Pooh! I daresay you know what's become of it."

"Yes," answered Jack calmly, at the same time fixing the other with a steady stare, "I *do* know what's become of it: at the present moment it's in its case in that cupboard there. Shall I show it you?"

The answer was so strange and unexpected that Raymond started; the meaning look in his cousin's eyes warned him that he was treading on dangerous ground. He had, however, gone too far to let the matter drop suddenly without any attempt to brazen out the situation.

"Humph!" he said; "I suppose you put it back yourself."

"I was the means of its being brought back. I found it in the pocket of an officer named Lawson who was killed in Egypt."

The withering tone and scornful curl of the lip was on the other side now. The visitor was fully aware of it, and winced as though he had been cut with a whip.

"Mr. Lawson had been stationed with the regiment at Melchester, and I happen to know how the watch came into his possession."

Raymond saw that he had rushed into a pitfall of his own making—he was entirely in his opponent's hands—and like the mean cur he was, immediately began to sue for forgiveness and terms of peace.

"Hush!" he cried, glancing at the door. "Don't say any more, the servants might hear. I'm very sorry I did it, but you know how it was; I was pushed for money, I say, you haven't told any one, have you?"

"No. Uncle John and Aunt Mabel know; though I don't think you need fear that they will let it go any further."

"That's all right," continued Raymond, in a snivelling tone. "I was badgered for money, and I really couldn't help it. I've been sorry enough since. I don't think I'll wait any longer, I'm in rather a hurry. Well, good-bye. And look here, old chap—I'm afraid I treated you rather badly; but we'll let bygones be bygones. I don't want it to get to the governor's ears, so you won't mention it, will you?"

Jack cast a contemptuous glance at the proffered hand, and put his own behind his back.

"No; I won't tell any one," he answered shortly, then turned on his heel, and that was his revenge.

And now the only person remaining of whom a last word might be said at parting, is our hero himself.

It was a balmy evening in that eternal summer that seemed to reign at Brenlands; and he and Queen Mab were walking slowly round the green lawn, while the swallows went wheeling to and fro overhead.

Fastened to her bunch of trinkets next the locket was a silver coin—the enlisting shilling, which Jack had never parted with since he first received it on that memorable morning at the Melchester barracks.

"Yes," said Aunt Mabel, "it was Queen Victoria's once, but now it's mine!"

"Well, I think I earned it," he answered, laughing.

"Perhaps you'd like to go and earn another?"

"No; I'm too happy where I am. Uncle John is awfully good to me. He couldn't be kinder if I were his own son."

"So you're content at last to stay at home and take what's given you?"

"Yes; I think I've settled down at last. Dear old Val said that the lane would turn some time, and so it has. My luck's changed."

"I think I'd put it down to something better than that," said Queen Mab, smiling. "Perhaps it is not all luck, but a little of yourself that has changed."

Jack laughed again, but made no attempt to deny the truth of the suggestion. Possibly he felt that what she said was right, and that not only in his surroundings, but also in his own heart, had come at last the long lane's turning.

## THE END.

www.ingramcontent.com/pod-product-compliance
Lightning Source LLC
Chambersburg PA
CBHW051132020726
47501CB00005B/1477